A Wedding Code

JACKI DELECKI

*To Karuna, my dear friend and plot partner,
who makes the challenges and frustrations
of story-making a joy!*

BOOKS BY JACKI DELECKI

THE CODE BREAKERS SERIES
Regency Suspense

A Code of Love

A Christmas Code

A Code of the Heart

A Cantata of Love

A Wedding Code

THE GRAYCE WALTERS SERIES
Romantic Suspense

An Inner Fire

Women Under Fire

Men Under Fire

Marriage Under Fire

A Wedding Code

PROLOGUE

Joseph Fouche paced in front of his desk, wearing a path in the deep Aubusson carpet. A servant, a damn sniveling servant, had delivered the message—Bonaparte didn't even have the balls to face him.

His failed attempt to assassinate King George had definitely threatened Bonaparte's sense of his rightful ascendency as Emperor of France. Bonaparte now thought of himself as a bloody royal. Didn't they just have a revolution to rid France of the bloodsucking aristos?

Fouche clenched his hands into tight fists, trying to restrain himself from acting on his seething rage.

With a single, careless note Bonaparte had stripped him of his position as the Minister of Police. With the same letter, Fouche became a very wealthy senator, thanks to the one million francs Bonaparte pillaged from the now-defunct Ministry of Police.

With one official act, Fouche's life's work was destroyed, in spite of his years of devoted support while Bonaparte ascended. This was how the emperor repaid loyalty.

He swore aloud. *"Après moi, le deluge."* After me, the flood.

He wouldn't be so easily bought off. His very lifeblood had been pumped into shaping the Ministry of Police.

Vengeance burned through his gut. Revenge thickened his blood and reverberated in his soul. He couldn't retaliate against Bonaparte, since he had to assume he was being watched—probably by men he, himself, had trained. Not yet. But eventually he would deliver justice to his new "monarch."

A man who planned methodically, Fouche never acted rashly. He would extract retribution and inflict pain. He was not considered the most feared man in France without good reason. He would spare no one. At this stage, what did he have to lose?

Thanks to his spies entrenched in the emperor's office, he knew this day was coming long before it happened, and he was prepared, prepared to behave as if he easily acquiesced to the emperor's wishes. His retribution would come much later.

Since he had built his own spider web of informants, and always planned years in advance, he was ready to retaliate. First in England and then in France. And first on his list for retribution—Lord Rathbourne, head of British spies, or, as he was formally known, Director of the Abchurch offices. Fouche needed to act quickly, before he was stripped of his power.

And after Rathbourne, the Marquis de Valmont. Valmont still lived because of Rathbourne. Valmont had been the mole who reported all of Fouche's failures to the emperor.

Fouche pulled the bell rope, and immediately the door was opened by his newly promoted assistant and assassin, Chasen, second in line since Valmont killed his top assassin. Oh, yes, Valmont would pay.

The lanky blond gave the appearance of a feckless youth, until you glimpsed his black, cold, soulless eyes. Fouche trusted no one other than a trained killer to control access to his office door.

"My minister, how may I be of service?" Chasen bowed.

"Are Valmont's nanny's children, Adrien and Lisette Dubois, still alive?"

"Yes, they remain in Bitche prison on charges of treason for assisting in the escape of the British spy Lord Kendal and Mademoiselle de Valmont."

"And their mother remains in the town of Berck?"

"Yes, my minister. She still lives. You were too lenient with the old woman."

Fouche laughed aloud. "No one has ever accused me of leniency." Maybe his new assistant would turn out to be entertaining. "Contact Commandant Maisonneuve to have them released under my command. You and they will be going to England."

"Monsieur?"

"You heard me correctly. You are in charge of the Dubois siblings."

"It is an honor." Chasen bowed again.

"The mademoiselle and monsieur are going to assist me in finishing what Anatole failed to achieve. They are to call upon their former mistress, Mademoiselle de Valmont, now Lady Kendal, and beg for her assistance. And remind them of my kindness toward their mother when I did not send her to Bitche fort, with its unforgiving dungeons."

Fouche sat behind his desk and wrote the orders for their release. "I'm sure they will appreciate that I've spared their mother from prison and the brutal Commandant Maisonneuve."

"When do you wish us to depart for England?"

Fouche handed him the paper. "You sail as soon as possible. Lady Rathbourne's baby is due any day."

"Yes, my minister." Chasen's boyish face registered no reaction to the mention that an infant was to be his next victim. Anatole had trained his successor well.

"Send in Maurice. He also travels to England. There is another matter to attend to."

No, he never acted rashly. He had prepared well for his final day as Minister of Police.

CHAPTER ONE

Miss Amelia Bonnington dropped the tangle of wedding ribbons and rushed into the morning room to assist Lady Henrietta Rathbourne. Amelia winced in sympathy at Hen's valiant but unsuccessful attempts to adjust her very large and very pregnant abdomen into a comfortable position on the settee.

Grabbing a pillow from a chair, Amelia tucked the cushion under Hen's swollen feet. "Darling, does this help?"

Not wanting to burden her best friend's sensitive feelings, Amelia tried hard not to stare at the massive round hump straining against Hen's morning gown. Amelia wasn't sure she wanted her body to ever grow and distort in such an uncomfortable manner. "Would another pillow behind your back help?"

"Nothing helps. I'm the size of a whale. It's not surprising that I'm having a big baby, since Cord is such a large man." Hen could barely wrap her arms around her middle.

Amelia didn't want to think about the imposing size of her fiancé, Lord Brinsley, and how large Derrick's babies would be. Although Amelia was inches taller than Henrietta, Derrick was a giant, the tallest and broadest man of her acquaintance.

Hen fanned her flushed face. "The entire family and staff are tiptoeing around me as if I might explode at any moment, like a Guy Fawkes firecracker."

It was true. The usually calm and composed Hen would tear up at the most unpredictable moments, leaving everyone around her baffled as to how to respond.

Amelia squeezed her friend's hand. "Everyone is concerned. And it's obvious that you're uncomfortable now that your time is near."

Henrietta stroked her abdomen in a protective, soothing circular motion. "Cord is constantly monitoring my growth. Every time he looks at me, I see him estimating the size of the baby. My enormous expansion has cracked his impenetrable confidence. He doesn't say anything, but I can see he is worried that the baby is too big for my small frame. And when my husband, the bravest and most fearless leader of our country, appears fearful, I feel a need to shelter him from what comes next."

Amelia shook her head. "But my dearest, you know Cord likes to be in control of everything and everyone. I'm sure he is struggling with this birthing business."

"My husband is used to bending all of England, even the king, to his will. His inability to control nature is driving him mad." Hen shifted on the settee, looking miserable.

Amelia jumped back up from her chair and repositioned the pillow under Hen's feet. "Does that help?"

Hen winced when Amelia moved her feet. "And Michael," she continued. "You know my brother can't hide a blasted feeling. It's all there on his face—fear and worry."

"It's normal for the men to worry. Besides, what other part can they play in the pregnancy?"

Hen rolled her bright green eyes toward the ceiling.

"Well, we know what part Cord played in the onset of my condition"

The childhood friends laughed together. And Amelia was relieved to see Hen able to muster some semblance of her usual wit.

"I still have days before the birth, according to Dr. Oglethorpe, which means I'll be able to attend your wedding."

Amelia didn't want to think about her best friend missing her wedding, which was but two days away. Hen refused to follow convention, and planned to attend despite her pregnant state, and Amelia supported her decision. She and Hen always planned to play a part in each other's weddings. They had shared their fantasies of romance, their future husbands, and dream weddings since they were eight years old.

"I'm so very weary of discussing the size of my abdomen and ankles. How are all the wedding details coming?"

"You don't have to pretend interest. I know you couldn't care less about colors, fabrics, or flowers."

"True. I was prodigiously grateful when you did everything for my wedding. How is Derrick faring with your need for perfection?"

Amelia had orchestrated Hen's, then Gwyneth's, and, most recently, Gabby's weddings. The brides were all dramatically in love and could scarcely be bothered with the kind of details that could turn a simple wedding into a glorious affair.

Their weddings were the talk of all London because of Amelia's eye for design. After Beau Brummel, Amelia was considered the highest arbiter of women's fashion. Although she hated the image of herself as another boring society woman whose only interest was fashion. She was an artist who saw color and shapes in everything around her.

Amelia grumbled. "I really don't need to have everything perfect."

Hen shifted on the settee and raised both eyebrows, accenting her round emerald eyes. "You changed the ribbon on my wedding dress at least five times to get the exact color of green moss. And the color of the hydrangeas and the candles… Should I go on?"

Amelia resisted pointing out that Hen looked magnificent on her wedding day because of Amelia's meticulous attention to every aspect of the event.

Hen fingered the sleeve of her gown. "And your protégé is worse. He couldn't be more persnickety."

"Pierpont is a wonderful help. He knows a great deal about fabrics, flowers, and proper etiquette." Amelia wanted to bite her tongue. She sounded like the snobbish society ladies she detested.

"I can't like him. There is something very cagey about him," Hen added.

"You've been listening to Derrick, haven't you?"

Hen shook her head. "Derrick hasn't said a word to me."

Amelia raised her eyebrows. "Are you sure?"

"Derrick barely speaks to me. I think he's intimidated by my size and my waddle."

Amelia snickered. "You might be right. It is rather startling to think that the two bravest men in England are afraid of one pregnant woman."

"Amelia, I don't care about Pierpont. But I do care about you. You did a remarkable job with all our weddings, but you were left exhausted and barely able to enjoy the festivities. I want you to enjoy your time as the bride."

Amelia had relished doing her close friends' weddings. But

for her own dream wedding, she envisioned a thousand ways she wanted it to be perfect. And therein lay the problem. She couldn't decide. Every small detail became exaggerated and daunting, and she debated with herself for hours over everything. And perhaps Hen was correct about Pierpont. He did seem to add to her anxiety by questioning every one of her decisions, making her second-guess herself.

Amelia gave a half-hearted laugh. "I'm driving Derrick mad. He might decide not to marry me."

"That giant, growling bear of a man only smiles and laughs when you're near. He isn't going to change his mind. He loves you."

Amelia felt her pale skin flush. The hardest part of being a redhead was when every tiny emotional response registered on your face for public consumption—no hiding any feelings. And didn't her brothers love to use her fair skin as a weapon against her?

"I keep asking him his opinion, but he doesn't have one. I believe he is actually color blind. I hope our children take after me when it comes to design."

Hen had been rubbing her hands in circles over her abdomen. "Oh, she's kicking again. I swear she is listening to our conversation." Hen reached for Amelia's hand. "Come feel her kick."

Hen and Amelia had decided when they were ten years old that their firstborn child would be female, against all societal expectations that they produce a firstborn male heir. They wanted their daughters to grow up to be best friends, as they had.

Hen placed Amelia's hand over her swollen belly, and the tiny foot kicked against Amelia's hand. Joy and wonder filled

Amelia's entire being. "Oh, my goodness, she is strong. She is going to make an exceptional cricket player."

Hen moaned suddenly, gripped her middle and threw her head back against the settee. "Her kicking started a painful birthing spasm."

Breathing through her mouth, with her eyes closed, Hen gripped Amelia's hand and whispered in something that sounded like Greek, "μὰ τὸν Δία."

Of course, only Hen would be swearing in Greek during her painful spasms.

Amelia stood helpless, watching Hen, pain etched across her forehead, her hold on Amelia's hand tightening into a death clasp. Anxiety pounded through Amelia. "My God, Hen, is the baby coming? What should I do?"

After a few interminable seconds, Hen's breathing slowed, and she opened her eyes and looked around.

Amelia released the tight breath she had been holding and squeezed Hen's hand. "I'm going to ring for Dr. Oglethorpe."

Lying back against the pillow, Hen gave a wan smile. "Please don't ring for him. Dr. Oglethorpe has reassured me that these spasms are a sign that my womb is preparing to have the baby." She swiped against her hair, further loosening the disarray of long auburn hair gathered at the back of her neck. "But the pain has definitely intensified."

"But if the pain is getting worse, shouldn't I summon him? This is why your husband has moved the doctor into your home."

Amelia's heart still pounded, and her knees were shaky from the fear coursing through her. Her mother had died in childbirth with her youngest brother.

"Amelia, you are not to tell anyone. Dr. Oglethorpe has

already told me these pains can go on for days. And please spare me—I don't want Cord or Michael hovering over me. They will drive me batty. It should be hours before we must notify my husband and my brother."

Hen bent over her abdomen and talked in a light, sing-song voice. "We're not going to permit the gentlemen to agitate us with their loud voices and commands, are we my darling?"

She wanted to argue with Hen, but lifelong loyalty held her back. "I'm going to ring for tea. You must have something to keep your strength up."

The door cracked open as Amelia moved toward the bell. Lisette, a new member to the Rathbourne household, peeked around the corner and asked, in her heavy French accent, "Madame?"

As if the last moment of pain and panic hadn't occurred, Hen smiled warmly at the petite French maid who had been hired to help with the baby. "Yes, Lisette, what is it?"

The young maid's eyes remained focused on the floor. "Mademoiselle Gabrielle." The maid's eyes jerked up in agitation. "Excusez-moi, my lady. Lady Kendal has arrived, and has asked if you are receiving visitors."

Hen made a brave attempt to sit in a more ladylike position. "Of course, show her in. But she's not a visitor, she's family."

When Lisette closed the door to summon Gabby, Hen flopped back on the pillows. "Oh, I hope Gabby has come alone. I would rather not see my brother, with his probing stares, until after the baby is born. Michael will realize immediately that I'm becoming uncomfortable. I can't keep anything from him."

"Your husband must have summoned him." Hen and her brother were both brilliant linguists who worked for the

Intelligence Office deciphering sensitive messages from France. "Michael will most likely be busy for a while."

"You must keep my brother and my husband out." Hen grabbed Amelia's hand. "Remember our promise."

"Of course, my dear, but at some point Cord will demand to see you." Amelia didn't want to stress Hen by telling her that there was no way Amelia could stop Hen's formidable husband. With four brothers, she was quite skilled at redirecting men, but no one could stop a determined Lord Rathbourne except his diminutive wife. And Cord loved Hen too much to be swayed by his wife's attempts to protect him.

"If there was any way to shield him from the labor, I'd wait and present the baby to him after. He will no doubt issue commands to everyone including poor Dr. Oglethorpe and our baby. He can be quite a tyrant."

The door opened quietly. Hen's new sister-in-law, a tiny Frenchwoman who always made Amelia feel gargantuan in comparison, waited in the doorway. The former Mademoiselle Gabrielle de Valmont had recently escaped France and Napoleon's plans to marry her to his brother for her fortune.

"Good afternoon, my ladies." Gabby curtsied properly before entering Henrietta's drawing room. Gabby's time spent hiding from Napoleon in a convent had influenced the young woman to behave with propriety despite Amelia and Gwyneth's attempts to cajole her into joining them in their "unseemly" antics.

Lisette remained at the door. "Shall I ring for a tea tray, Madame?"

Amelia answered when Hen flinched and closed her eyes. "Yes, Lisette, please bring tea. And if Lady Gwyneth, Lord Rathbourne's sister, arrives, please escort her to the morning room."

Unaware of Hen's discomfort, Gabby walked over to stand next to Amelia and said, in a light, melodic voice, "Lisette told me this morning how very happy she is to be at Rathbourne House. It was most generous of you and Lord Rathbourne to permit my meme's children to become part of your household. Lisette loves babies. She will be very helpful, just like my dear nanny."

Sensing her friend's distress, Amelia rearranged the pillow under Hen's feet and fluffed the one behind her back.

Repositioned, Hen exhaled softly and rubbed her belly in light circles. "Please, both of you, be seated."

Amelia didn't want to sit. She needed to keep moving to get rid of the fidgety, restless feeling overtaking her. She studied Hen's face, saw her try to mask her pain for her gentle sister-in-law. The tense lines around Hen's mouth had softened during Gabby's distracting conversation.

Taking a slow breath, Amelia sat next to Gabby on the diminutive, gilded ladies' chairs facing the settee.

"It is the least we could do for the family. It is because of Lisette's mother that you and my brother were able to escape France," Hen said.

Like all the ladies' husbands, Amelia's fiancé, Derrick, was involved in the war against France. The men tried to make little of the brutality of their work, but the arrival of Lisette and her brother had brought the harsh reality into their homes.

"I still can't believe Lissette and Adrien were sent to the worst prison in France for helping you and Michael escape." Amelia didn't share that Derrick was surprised that the youths hadn't been executed for their treason. Derrick had not told Amelia, but she overheard him discussing it with Cord.

Derrick, like all the men, tried to protect their women.

Amelia didn't want to be protected. She discovered a French spy ring headquartered in a modiste's. She had skills that could assist Derrick's fight against France. She didn't want to be consigned to being yet another aristocratic, pampered, and coddled female.

"I still feel terrible about what she and her brother have suffered, but I had no one else to turn to. And Michael was so ill." Gabby's voice wavered.

"It isn't your fault that Fouche is evil and is willing to make innocents suffer. And remember what the consequences would be if your meme hadn't helped you. Michael wouldn't have come home." Hen wiped away the tears streaking her face.

"And now Lisette and Adrien are out of France and away from Fouche," Amelia chimed in, to turn Hen's thoughts away from the possibility of losing her brother.

Gabby nodded. "Yes, Michael reminds me that they've been freed, and will never suffer again. I'm sorry that my meme is in France while her children are now in England. But she refuses to leave France. When the war ends, I'm sure Lisette and Adrien will return to her." Gabby straightened the morning blue walking dress Amelia had selected for her. "Lisette and Adrien have reassured me that Fouche considered their mother too old to be sent to prison."

"Well, I guess there is some goodness in Fouche." Amelia snorted. She wanted to comment, "Devil a bit," as her brothers would have.

Hen closed her eyes again and gripped the side of the settee, saying under her breath, "μὰ τὸν Δία."

Gabby stared at Hen, her cornflower blue eyes widening and her mouth gaping.

Amelia jumped up to stand next to Hen. "She is starting labor."

Gabby muttered in French. "Oh, mon Dieu."

Trying not to disturb Hen—who now was panting through her open mouth, her face again contorted in agony—Gabby tiptoed closer to Amelia and whispered behind her hand, "Shouldn't we call Dr. Oglethorpe? And Lord Rathbourne?"

Hen groaned. "No. Not yet. You promised, Amelia."

CHAPTER TWO

Lord Derrick Brinsley lifted the hefty, upholstered mahogany chair from in front of the fireplace and carried it to a spot opposite his superior's desk.

His manly parts still ached from his morning visit with Aunt Mabel. Balancing on the tiny gilt chair, feigning interest in his aunt's recitation of all the details of his upcoming wedding, was worse than being interrogated by the French. Thank God for the chairs in Lord Rathbourne's office that could accommodate his large frame.

All of London's morning and drawing rooms were filled with the fashionable French-designed chairs that couldn't fit an average sized man, which he hadn't been since he was twelve years old. It was bad enough that his entire life was spent fighting against the tyranny of the French emperor, without also having to suffer from French fashion in his leisure time.

He didn't want to think about the French and their fashions. His fiancée's French fashion protégé, Monsieur Pierpont, was a large pain in Derrick's arse. The man was always eyeing him as though Derrick didn't measure up to his expectations as a man of fashion. Derrick didn't give a damn about fashion, but, since Amelia did care, he tried to give more attention to his clothing.

His valet understood Derrick's tastes were simple, and honored the man's expectation that his jackets would accommodate movement instead of trussing him up like a Christmas goose.

Derrick didn't trust Pisspot, as he called the weasely man. There was something devious about him. It was more than the haughty Frenchman's fashion intolerance or his own jealousy that the designer spent a great deal of time with Amelia that made Derrick suspicious.

Derrick didn't want to raise Amelia's concerns, since she was already stressed by the upcoming wedding. But that didn't prevent Derrick from having his contacts in France investigate Pierpont's background. Derrick also asked his Aunt Mabel to verify that Pierpont was truly the nephew of Lady Wadsworth. According to Lady Wadsworth, his parents were guillotined, and she had been working for years to bring her beloved nephew to England. In these times, it was prudent to be careful, and Derrick was more than careful with Amelia.

"Pray, be seated…" Lord Cordelier Rathbourne raised one dark eyebrow in his familiar sardonic manner. "…whenever you're ready."

He'd been so lost in thought Derrick hadn't realized he was still holding the mahogany chair aloft.

Rathbourne, the highly-respected head of Abchurch Office, wasn't prone to joking or laughter, but as Derrick spent more time with the man, he learned to appreciate Rathbourne's droll sense of humor. There was a lighter side to the man all of England was depending on to save their country.

Derrick noted Rathbourne's loosened, pristine white cravat, the only jarring note in his de-rigueur perfect gentlemen's morning attire. It was evidence of the lack of sleep that had darkened the skin under Rathbourne's eyes to almost the same ebony shade as his eyebrows and hair, and heightened the weariness clear on his harsh, angled face.

"I've just received word. Fouche was officially removed from his position as head of the Ministry of Police. His office and staff have been disbanded."

"So Fouche's plot to kill King George pushed Napoleon's tolerance for Fouche's machinations?" Derrick asked.

Rathbourne tugged on his cravat. "Most likely Fouche's lack of respect for royalty touched too close to Napoleon's newly acquired royal blood."

"Royal blood, my arse!" Derrick choked out. "I assume all of Napoleon's actions are driven by his need for adulation and power."

"That's a given. But Napoleon's obsession with power works to our benefit in this case, since Fouche is out and Valmont has returned to France as our agent."

"How long will it take us to untangle all the plots and subterfuges Fouche has set in place?" Derrick asked.

"Napoleon has disbanded the Ministry of Police, but the men loyal to Fouche will not simply disappear. For years, he has been building a network of spies, assassins, and thugs. We must assume Napoleon will utilize the resources for his own villainous purposes."

The men sat in silence, each pondering possible sources of the next threat against England.

Rathbourne ran his hand back and forth along his jaw. "Fouche will not step down passively. He'll continue to be a threat that we must not underestimate. And he will certainly pursue Valmont and Kendal, the men who uncovered his plot and set in motion his dismissal."

"I do not have your trusting nature," Derrick said.

Rathbourne barked out a laugh. "Trusting!"

Derrick spent a great deal of time with Rathbourne since his engagement to Rathbourne's wife Henrietta's best friend. And, like Derrick, Rathbourne was a large, silent man who didn't trust easily. Their suspicious natures were an important asset in their work.

"Can you trust Valmont to not kill Fouche while he is in France? His revenge would ruin our strategy to use him as a double agent."

"Of course I cannot trust Valmont. His sister was nearly abducted, and he was shot and left for dead. I cannot fault him for seeking revenge."

"Then how could you allow Valmont to return to France?"

"Expediency. Valmont, as a former marquis-turned-spy, will hopefully learn Napoleon's timetable for invading England. We know Napoleon is assembling forces and building boats in Eastern France. I had to take a calculated risk."

"A calculation that there is a greater likelihood that Valmont will return to England with intelligence rather than kill Fouche."

Rathbourne nodded. "Before Valmont left for France, he reassured me that killing Fouche would be too simple. Valmont plans to make Fouche suffer for terrorizing his sister. If anyone threatened my sister or my wife, I'd be hard-pressed to spare the criminal. Besides, Fouche has never exhibited any honor in the game of spies. He is willing to prey on the weak to achieve his goals. Thus, I can appreciate Valmont's need for justice, as you well do too?"

Derrick stared at the deep burgundy tones in the Aubusson rug at his feet. "Not many believed in me beyond you and Sir Ramsay. I will always be in your debt."

Derrick was ostracized by society after he broke all social taboos by supposedly eloping with his brother's fiancée. Everyone but Rathbourne's predecessor, Sir Ramsay, and then Rathbourne himself, had assumed the worst and questioned his honor. Derrick never learned how the men discovered the truth, but he was recruited to work for the Abchurch offices while he remained a social outcast.

"Yes, we all had reputations that Sir Ramsay looked past when he called upon us to serve our country."

Rathbourne had a reputation of being reckless, wild, and a rake of the first order, until he met Lady Henrietta. Derrick had insight into the man that few outside the family circle would believe—the dogged, uncompromising man would do anything for his tiny, brilliant wife.

"Are you worried about the threat to your brother-in-law, or possibly his wife?"

"Of course. Henrietta would never forgive me if anything happened to her brother or Lady Kendal. Since he returned from France, Kendal has been well guarded since he is our code breaker. Nothing will happen to Henrietta's brother or Gabby on my watch."

Derrick shifted in his chair and cleared his throat. His boss was a prickly sort who didn't like interference. Derrick hesitated, knowing he was stepping outside the boundaries of his position. But his duty to raise the issue outweighed the possible repercussions. "Speaking of ears everywhere, don't you think it's too much of a coincidence that two French emigres with family connections to Valmont and his sister are now in your household?"

Rathbourne's eyes narrowed on Derrick's face, but Derrick refused to be intimidated by his superior's scrutiny. "I couldn't say no to the family who was pivotal in saving my brother-in-law's life. But that doesn't mean that they aren't being closely monitored. I would never risk strangers to join my household with Lady Henrietta, Edward, and Uncle Charles.

"I assumed as much." Derrick grinned. "I also know how hard it is to say no to a redhead." Derrick flashed on agreeing to wear an embroidered burgundy vest on his wedding day because Amelia wanted him to match the flowers. Something he would admit to no one.

"Henrietta isn't a redhead like Amelia—my wife can be very reasonable." Rathbourne leaned back in his chair. "But since the pregnancy she seems to have acquired a few redheaded traits."

Derrick wasn't offended by the reference to Amelia's bright red hair and her matching fiery personality. He loved her passionate response to his lovemaking, her competitive streak, her athleticism in cricket, and her defense of anyone suffering. He loved Amelia, and the light she brought into his dark past, as Lady Henrietta had done for Rathbourne.

"I somehow feel like I should take offense on Amelia's behalf." Derrick raised his eyebrow in imitation of his superior.

"I meant no insult to Amelia, who is as steady as my wife."

Rathbourne rubbed his chin. "Now, my sister…although not a redhead…"

The door swung open, and Rathbourne's Aunt Euphemia marched into the room with a footman scurrying after her.

In a stern, no-nonsense voice, she addressed Rathbourne. "You must go to your wife. Her time has arrived."

Rathbourne bolted out of his chair. "Now?" He strode to the door, then paused in the doorjamb. "She has started having birthing pains?"

"She's been laboring all morning," Aunt Euphemia announced.

Rathbourne's voice was low and intense. "And why am I just being notified?"

Derrick stood by his chair, unsure of his role.

Aunt Euphemia followed into the hallway. "Because I'm the only one not bound to silence by a promise to Henrietta not to tell you. She has made Amelia and Dr. Oglethorpe promise secrecy. You were not to be told until she was almost ready to deliver the baby."

"Of all the misguided, harebrained ideas." Rathbourne threw up his arms. "Why in the hell wouldn't she tell me?" Derrick had never witnessed Rathbourne as having anything other than complete control of himself, typically slow to react to any disaster.

"I'm going to kill Oglethorpe for allowing my wife to be in labor without notifying me."

Aunt Euphemia grabbed Rathbourne's arm as he turned to ascend the stairs. "That is exactly why Henrietta didn't want you to know. She believes your concern will make you unreasonable."

"Me? Unreasonable?" Rathbourne's voice echoed in the hallway.

Aunt Euphemia patted his arm. "Of course I reassured both Henrietta and Dr. Oglethorpe that you would be able to control your emotions, since you are fully aware that a calm, reassuring husband will be the best possible support for Henrietta."

"My God. I can control my emotions in every extreme situation. I've faced my death more times than I want to remember. Why should my wife have such little faith in me?"

A high-pitched shout of "μὰ τὸν Δία" echoed in the marble hallway.

"Henrietta!" Rathbourne rasped his wife's name as if all the air had had been knocked from his lungs. His ruddy complexion turned ashen. He took the stairs two at a time up the long, winding stairwell to the upper floor.

"What is Lady Henrietta shouting?"

"According to Amelia, she is swearing in Ancient Greek. She is cursing the Greek God Zeus." Aunt Euphemia shook her head vehemently, tilting the fuchsia turban perched on her head to the side like a listing sailboat. "Balderdash. I'm too old for such drama. Get me a brandy, my boy."

Derrick was only called "boy" by his Aunt Mabel, and now Aunt Euphemia. "Of course." He walked toward the older woman. "May I help you to a chair?"

"I might be old, but I'm not an invalid." She paraded to the other mahogany chair in front of the fireplace.

Unlike most ladies of her age and position, she didn't sit on the edge of the chair with her ankles crossed daintily and her hands folded in her lap. She leaned back and crossed her legs as a gentleman would.

"You better pour yourself one, too."

Derrick stared at Aunt Euphemia. Having just spent the morning with his Aunt Mabel, he was used to the vagaries and whims of women of "an age." They showed no discretion in meddling in the personal matters of anyone who was younger than they. Which of course was all of London.

"I convinced Amelia to leave Henrietta's side long enough to have some tea in my drawing room. She has refused to leave her friend, because of the promise they made as young girls. But since she is an unmarried woman, I imagine the birthing process will be a bit of a shock, even to someone of Amelia's fortitude. You must go to her. She will need your support and comfort."

Derrick's stomach lurched. My God, Amelia was with Lady Henrietta. His hands trembled when he poured the brandy. He knew nothing of births, or the pain women went through to deliver a baby. How was he to calm her?

Obviously, Aunt Euphemia, a spinster, had no more experience than he did with the business of birthing. A high-pitched screech filled the room despite the partially closed door, and Derrick's heart slammed against his chest at the daunting sound.

The old gel had gone into the French mess and rescued women and children from the guillotine, but still a look of shock and fear spread across her wrinkled face. Did she recognize the same expression he was sure must be evident on his own face?

Aunt Euphemia threw back the brandy like a seasoned drinker and then pushed her listing turban upright to carefully inspect his face. "Do you know that Amelia's mother died in childbirth with the arrival of her youngest brother? I am to understand it was a traumatic experience for the sensitive young girl. She will need you to be strong for her during this time of her closest friend's labor."

Derrick poured himself a hefty shot and, like the old gel, threw back the brandy in hopes the alcohol would quell his rising panic. He relished danger and a bloody good fight, but the idea of consoling Amelia during Lady Henrietta's labor caused his heart to hammer against his chest the way it did when he tossed a man across a pub.

The brandy warmed him as it went down his gullet but didn't stop the sick feeling.

Since he wasn't a man to prevaricate, he placed his glass on the side table, despite the temptation to have another shot to steady himself. "I must go to her. May I top off your glass before I leave?"

Aunt Euphemia cackled in a deep, manly voice. "Aren't you the polite one under that giant, brawny body? You can't top off something that is gone. You go. I don't want Amelia alone. I can serve myself."

And, like Rathbourne, he bounded up the hallway staircase, taking two at a time.

CHAPTER THREE

Derrick reached the top of the enormous stairwell and paused. The long hall stretched and twisted past endless closed doors. He had never visited the family's private quarters, and had no idea which door opened to Aunt Euphemia's drawing room. He definitely did not want to blunder into the labor room. He stood waiting for some clue.

Brompton, the family retainer, his white hair combed severely back, came around the corner. "My lord, may I assist you?"

"Much obliged, Brompton. I'm in search of Miss Amelia."

"Of course. I just brought a tea tray to Miss Amelia in Lady Beaumont's drawing room." Brompton gestured with his arm. "This way."

Brompton moved more slowly today, as if a weight pressed on his shoulders. Amelia told him the Bromptons had acted like grandparents to the young Henrietta and her family after the untimely death of their parents. "How is Lady Henrietta?"

Brompton kept his slow pace down the hallway. "My wife is with her, and has reassured me that Lady Henrietta is progressing as expected during this difficult time." The man delivered the message in his usual formal, precise manner.

A high-pitched cry rent the air.

The eerie sound grated on Derrick's nerves, revving him into high alert, as if he were trailing a deadly French assassin.

The momentary silence was followed by a loud, angry shout. "Oglethorpe, I'm going to rip you limb from limb if you don't get this baby out."

"Oh, my," Brompton said. "Not exactly what I would have expected from his lordship. But these are stressful times."

Both men stood, unable to move, as hushed voices responded to the outburst. Derrick waited, his senses vigilant for the next outburst.

Brompton's face was mainly in the shadows, but Derrick could see white tightness around the butler's mouth.

"I'm sure Lady Henrietta will be fine." Derrick regretted the inadequacy of his reassurance, and prayed he was correct.

"Thank you, my lord." Brompton stared straight ahead as he opened the door. "Is there anything else you'll require, sir?"

"No, thank you." Derrick paused before entering the room. No wonder Amelia was upset. His heart beat double-time because of his the close proximity to Lady Henrietta's distress and the panic in Cord's shouts.

He might be a spy who thrived on danger and menace, but he was dismayed by the fear that permeated the house and its inhabitants. He straightened his shoulders and braced himself to do his duty. Nothing could have prepared him for the sight of Amelia attempting to push the heavy mahogany settee across the room. The lonely bewilderment in her eyes was a blow to his gut.

He had never seen his vivacious Amelia, the competitive athlete, the darling of the drawing rooms across London, looking lost and vulnerable. Her hair was coming out of its pins, and her fashionable dress was rumpled and spotted.

He lost all his trepidations upon seeing her and walked quickly to her side. "Amelia, why are you moving the furniture?"

She glanced up as if she didn't recognize him. Her normally bright eyes were wide and dimmed in fear. "I believe the room is unbalanced, and if the settee is moved to a ninety-degree angle to the table…"

He lifted her into his arms and pulled her against his chest, holding her tight. "Darling, everything is going to be fine."

He felt her trembling against him when he sat on the settee, settling her on his lap. With her face pressed against his chest, she spoke in quiet desperation. "There is so much blood."

Derrick's heart plummeted. God, that didn't sound like a good sign. Could it be normal to lose blood?

"And the pain. I didn't know how to help her."

He rocked her gently and kissed the top of her head—lost for words, wanting everything to be better, but not knowing how to make it so.

"I promised I'd be there, but I'm no help to Hen during this awful time."

He held her securely along the nape of her neck and spoke gently. "You're doing what's important. Being by her side is a help to Lady Henrietta."

Amelia shook her head against his hold. "No, she didn't even seem to know I was there, or hear anything I said."

Derrick knew nothing about the pain of birthing, but he'd experienced enough serious injuries to understand overwhelming pain. A vivid memory flashed through his mind of the last time he was shot by Fouche's man while trying to help Kendal escape France. The agony of the bullet lodged in his thigh as he gave chase, his vision tunneling, and the inability to do anything but focus on his mission: to protect Kendal.

He stroked her soft hair. "She knew you were there. She had to save all her energy."

"How do you know about birthing?" Amelia looked up. Tears pooled in her smoky amethyst eyes.

He tucked an errant, fiery lock behind her ear. "I know nothing about birthing, but I do know a lot about pain. Lady Henrietta has to focus on the birth of her baby." He chose not to mention that probably she could only focus on keeping the pain at bay.

Derrick didn't loosen his hold on Amelia, and pressed her head back against his chest. He ran his hand down her spine, enjoying holding her, keeping her safe. He didn't think Amelia could help at this point, but he understood her need, and admired her loyalty to her friend.

"Her husband is with her right now. And Mrs. Brompton. You'll be of no use to her if you exhaust yourself. You need to have some tea and sustenance." If only he could convince Amelia to go outside, away from the house and the screaming, but he doubted she would abandon her friend.

Amelia shook her head against his shoulder. He could barely hear her and leaned closer. She mumbled like a rejected child. "I'm not hungry."

That was surprising, since Amelia, unlike most women, ate like a man. No dainty bites for her. Probably a reflection of growing up in a household with her brothers.

"I have to be with her. I promised to keep Cord and Michael away."

"Where is Kendal? I haven't seen him since he arrived."

Amelia fingered the folds of Derrick's cravat. "Gabby took

her husband to the folly to distract him away from the house."

"Devious woman!" Derrick took Amelia's hand and pressed kisses to her knuckles. "Will you promise to distract me soon?"

Derrick felt Amelia's intake of breath, and his muscles clenched in response. Since they announced their wedding, Amelia and Derrick were scarcely ever alone.

"Our wedding is only two days away."

It couldn't come soon enough for Derrick. He missed his Amelia, her affection. A man who prided himself in his experience with women, Derrick was flummoxed by the changes in his fiancée. His laughing, spirited fiancée was overwrought over the wedding, and unwilling to permit him to use his best methods of helping her relieve the tension. Of course, his experiences with women were mainly in the boudoir, not negotiating a wedding with endless decisions of color choices, music, or hardly-known relatives demanding to be included.

Amelia shifted her weight on his lap, and he tried to tamp down his physical reaction to her rounded derriere pressing against him. "Derrick, will you want to be with me when I'm in labor?"

He tried to focus on what Amelia asked. But his brain was muddled. He was still thinking about being with Amelia, with no restraints on their lovemaking. What had she asked? She wanted him with her during labor.

"Hen didn't want Cord in the room because she knew he'd be worried and take it out on dear Dr. Oglethorpe."

"It was bit unrealistic of Lady Henrietta to think she could keep her husband away."

Amelia toyed with the buttons on his waistcoat. "But most

husbands don't want to be in the room. I can understand. It is quite messy and scary."

Derrick couldn't stop the images of Amelia in labor, in pain and bleeding. He didn't want her to suffer. He loved her and wanted to protect her from all upsetting things, but he knew she wanted children as much as he. Amelia screaming—the risk of her dying.

He had to rethink his feelings about the birthing process. He couldn't get past the fact that he might lose Amelia. No child was worth that.

Amelia leaned back against his chest. "The baby is enormous. And she is a tiny woman."

Derrick didn't have any response. When he saw Lady Henrietta two days ago, she was the size of a battleship. And she wobbled awkwardly under the weight of her impressive middle.

"You're so much bigger than Cord." He was thinking the same thing. He didn't want her to have a baby who was too large, who might kill her in childbed. Women, like her mother, died in childbirth. He couldn't lose Amelia. He finally felt his life had purpose with her, planning their future.

Another shriek filled the room despite the heavy doors.

His hold tightened around her. "You're right. The baby will be too big for you. We can't… We won't have children."

Amelia pulled away to look up into his eyes. "What?"

"I can't lose you. We won't have children. I never want you to suffer."

Amelia watched his face, her eyes filled with concern. "Oh, darling, of course, we will." She wrapped her arms around his middle. He was supposed to be comforting Amelia, but instead she was reassuring him.

"I mean it, Amelia. I couldn't bear for you to hurt like this."

His voice turned ragged from the tumultuous feelings overwhelming him.

"But I want children. Remember, you promised me my own cricket team."

At the sound of someone approaching the door, Amelia pushed against his chest and got to her feet.

CHAPTER FOUR

Amelia brushed at her crumpled dress and tried to pin her falling hair back into place.

Derrick came up behind her, standing close—so close that she could feel the heat radiating off him. "Darling, let me help with your hair." She recognized the desire in his husky voice, and had turned to chide him to behave himself when the door swung open.

Edward, Hen's youngest brother, and Gus, a stocky Labrador retriever and the boy's faithful companion, rushed into the room. Mr. Marlowe, Edward's tutor, was supposed to have occupied Edward and Gus with a walk into town. She had spoken to Marlowe herself. Edward needed to be away from the distressing household.

"I heard Hen scream." His high-pitched voice cracked with emotion. "Why is my sister screaming?"

An explosion of long-suppressed and painful memories racked Amelia's body. No child should have to hear its mother screaming out of control.

The fear in Edward's voice mobilized her, and yanked her out of her own misery. She dashed to him and pulled him into her arms. "Hen is doing great, but there is always discomfort in childbirth."

Edward threw his arms around Amelia's waist. Gus, who

usually stalked the tea tray, instead leaned against Edward's leg and crooned a low, keening sound of misery.

"Your sister is very strong. She will not allow a little unpleasantness to keep her from having her baby. Trust me, before you know it, she'll be back deciphering codes with you and Michael."

Derrick bent to reassure Gus. He rubbed the dog's blocky head. "It's okay, big fella."

Edward clung to Amelia. His desperate need quashed her raw memories. She was used to her two younger brothers looking up to her as their mother, and she couldn't help responding to Edward's hurt.

"What happened to your tutor? I thought you all were walking into town."

Edward shook his head, but didn't loosen his hold. "He has no orienteering skills. It isn't even a challenge for me and Gus to lose him. We came to find out why we were suddenly sent on an excursion."

Like his older siblings, Edward was too intelligent to be easily fooled by her machinations.

Amelia rubbed Edward's sandy-blond hair, the exact color of his older brother's. "Well, I'm not sure what punishment Mr. Marlowe will mete out for you and Gus for this latest transgression. But since babies can take a long time coming, I think we should work on your pitching."

"Cricket? You mean it? You'll play with me?" Edward relaxed his grip on her waist. And Gus's ears pointed on alert, and his tail thumped with pleasure.

"But should we leave Hen?" Edward bent down to his dog, wrapping his arm around the dog's wide neck. "She might need me and Gus."

"I think we have plenty of time to practice and still be ready to welcome the new baby."

"My mother told me that I took the longest to arrive because I was the biggest of all her babies."

"There, you see?" Hen had shared her worries about how Edward would feel about the baby following so soon after Michael's wedding. "You already have something in common with the baby, since I think he or she is going to be big as well."

Considering the effort it would take for Hen to push out her large baby, Amelia needed to get Edward outside quickly.

"You and Gus get the equipment, and Derrick and I will join you."

Edward stood and looked back and forth between her and Derrick. "You promise not to take too long?"

"Of course not. Why would you think that? I must inform Mrs. Brompton where we'll be."

"Michael always promises he won't be long, but he and Gabby play kissy. It always takes the longest time. Isn't that so, Gus?"

Gus tipped his head to one side, and wagged harder.

"Of all the outrageous things to say, Edward Michael Harcourt." Amelia had to suppress a grin with Derrick's chuckle.

Derrick bumped the boy on the shoulder. "It won't be long, Edward, and you'll be wanting to play kissy-face, too."

"Ugh! Gus and I are remaining bachelors." Edward looked around Derrick. "The tea tray. Exactly what Gus and I need before we play cricket. We had to walk a really long way to double back after leaving Mr. Marlowe in the woods."

"Why don't you take the food outside with you? That way you'll have everything ready for us to play," Amelia said.

Edward had no difficulty foregoing the tea time ritual of sitting down and demonstrating polite behavior. He rushed to the tea tray, popped a small biscuit into his mouth, and threw another to Gus, who caught the flying treat with a snap of his jaws.

Edward repeated the stunt with two more biscuits before piling bread and fruit into his hands.

Amelia didn't utter a word of reproof since she wanted the boy and dog away from the house.

Derrick ambled over to Edward. "Need any help, old man?"

"Can you open the door for me and Gus?" Edward spoke around a mouth stuffed with biscuit.

"Of course." Derrick popped a biscuit into his own mouth and, like Edward, tossed one to Gus. No wonder the dog was stout. If Mrs. Brompton ever found out her favorite biscuits were feeding Gus, there would be hell to pay.

Edward walked out into the hall with Gus at his side in a strategic position to catch any falling morsels "You won't take too long?" The quiver in his voice betrayed his worry.

"Me? Take too long for a chance to play cricket?" She raised her eyebrows in mocking query, and the boyish grin spreading across Edward's face was worth the lie.

Edward and Gus took off in a run down the hall. Watching Edward's retreating figure, Amelia prayed that Hen and her baby would be safe. She refused to contemplate any other outcome.

As if he understood her dark thoughts, Derrick wrapped his arms around her from behind. "You were remarkable with Edward. I didn't think I could fall more in love, but what you did just now has captured my deepest admiration. Miss Amelia

Bonnington, you are an amazing woman, and I am a very fortunate man."

Amelia leaned into his strong chest, enjoying his heat, his warm words, and the feeling of safety. "I didn't want him to experience what I did. I might not be able to help Hen at this moment, but she would not want Edward to be alone and afraid as I was."

Derrick tightened his hold. "I wish I had known you then. I would have protected you."

Amelia snuggled closer and stroked his large hands, which were resting on her abdomen. "My protector. I'm glad you're here with me now."

"Always." Derrick's deep voice whispered against her ear, sending shivers down her spine.

Derrick made it easy to forget her fear and worries. "I promised to distract you, but you…" Need coursed through her. "You are very good at befuddling me, and we promised Edward we would not dally."

Derrick placed open kisses along her neck. "Amelia, I promise to more than befuddle you tomorrow night."

Amelia's knees weakened. "Derrick, play fair. I need to check on Hen and inform Mrs. Brompton where I will be."

She turned in his arms. "Play fair? I'm trying, but I'm a desperate man who needs his fiancée." He brushed her bottom lip with his thumb. "Do you want me to accompany you?"

"Although I appreciate the offer, I think Edward needs you more right now. Would you go help him set up? He's a very clever boy, and he understands what is happening. Hen has been a mother to him, and he is frightened."

He kissed her gently on the lips. "Go quickly, then. Edward, Gus, and I will be waiting. I can't wait to play cricket with you."

"Really? You never seemed to care about cricket."

"It gives me an opportunity to glimpse my bride-to-be's ankles. I'm that desperate."

Amelia couldn't believe she was smiling as she hurried down the hall to Hen's room.

CHAPTER FIVE

Derrick and Ashworth waited for Rathbourne in the library. Viscount Ashworth, Rathbourne's closest friend, looked as tired as Derrick felt. His blond hair was tousled, and his shirt was wrinkled, as if he had thrown on the same one from last night.

Neither men slept much while awaiting the birth of Lord Charles Cordelier Ormond Beaumont, the next Earl of Rathbourne. Comforting their wives during the grueling labor had taken the stuffing out of both men. Birthing apparently required the same skillset as a soldier—endurance, strength, and courage.

And Ashworth had his hands full with his wife, Rathbourne's younger sister, a rambunctious woman who had threatened to punch the harried Dr. Oglethorpe.

"How is Lady Gwyneth this morning?"

"My wife has exhausted herself, and was not happy at my insistence that she rest this morning. I'm expecting her to arrive at any moment." Ash laughed.

"Would she have actually punched Dr. Oglethorpe as she threatened?" Derrick had difficulty not laughing at the memory of Ash's wife, hands fisted in the air, poised to harm the esteemed physician. Fortunately, Ashworth intervened before she could follow through with expressing the fear and helplessness everyone was feeling while Lady Henrietta labored way into the night, straining to push the large babe out.

"My wife is a Rathbourne. It was to be expected. And, as you might have noticed, Aunt Euphemia was ready to join in the fray. Be grateful you didn't marry into a family of spirited women."

As the hours passed into the night, Derrick hated watching his feisty Amelia withdraw, as she must have done as a bewildered young girl during the labor of her mother.

The footman opened the door, and the father himself walked into his office.

"My God, Cord, you look like you're the one who labored through the night." Ash laughed.

Derrick searched Rathbourne's face, noting his eyes were both puffy and encircled by a rim of redness.

"How is Lady Henrietta?" Derrick asked. Amelia told him the worry wasn't over yet, because some women died from infection after the baby was born. He really wished he could return to his blissful state of ignorance concerning womanly matters.

"Surprisingly chipper this morning." Rathbourne ran his hand over his hair. "I'd rather be tortured than have my wife…" He seated himself at the desk, shaking his head. "After what she endured…"

Derrick sympathized. He hadn't slept after he took Amelia home, asleep in the carriage. After the long and worrisome night, Amelia's exhaustion vanished when she held the wee babe in her arms. Her fear had transformed into pure delight as she cooed at the baby, her face wreathed in joy. Derrick wished he could as blithely forget the risk involved in birthing.

Ash leaned back in an indolent, devil-may-care manner, posturing as if the men hadn't witnessed him gently soothing his wife on his lap while she wept loudly after the birth. "Let's face it—there is a reason women have babies and men don't."

Derrick caught the hint of a smile on his superior's face before he pulled out the papers from his desk. "Let's get back to the business we men are good at—fighting a war. Despite all the excitement of last night, Napoleon is still planning to invade England."

"Hear! Hear! To men and their limited talents." Ashworth raised his hand in an imaginary toast.

"Brinsley, any word from Morlaix?"

Derrick spent time in the small town of Brittany after he saw to the safe return of Kendal to England. He was able to do his reconnaissance, despite his size, because he didn't stand out in a fishing town populated with descendants of hulking Norman invaders.

"The rumors are true. Napoleon is gathering an invasion force on the Coast of Brittany, preparing to invade Ireland. My informant reports that Bernard MacSheehy, adjutant general in Napoleon's army, has been tasked with formation of a legion of men, including the Irish rebels."

Ashworth bolted upright. "Napoleon is recruiting the Irish rebels for his army?"

"It is a brilliant strategy. The Legion's purpose is to engage the Irish against the English, which won't be difficult, considering our history with Ireland," Derrick explained.

Rathbourne nodded. "Go on."

"With the Irish help, the French then can invade us by land in addition to the sea assault," Derrick concluded.

With the French's continued recruitment of the

disenfranchised Irish, Derrick hoped he wouldn't be sent undercover into Ireland, away from his soon-to-be bride. But this was wartime, and everyone had to make sacrifices.

The door swung open, and Mr. Marlowe, a reedy young man, rushed into the library. He held the door, waiting for the footman to depart.

Rathbourne's expression changed into one of appalled shock. "Not now, Marlowe."

"Sir, I have something of the utmost importance. I don't want to alert the household, because I don't want Lady Rathbourne to learn of it from any of the maids. I feel the stress would be too much for my lady." He spoke rapidly, without pausing for breath.

Rathbourne jerked upright and stood. "What are you talking about Marlowe? You're trying my patience. If this is about one of Edward's hijinks…"

The young man gulped, bobbing the prominent Adam's apple in his narrow throat. "No, my lord. Master Edward is missing."

"What? How can Edward have gone missing?" Cord tapped his finger on the top of his desk, glaring at the young tutor.

Ash stood and approached Mr. Marlowe. "Are you sure he's missing and not pulling one of his tricks?"

"No, Lord Ashworth. His bed has not been slept in, and neither he nor Gus has eaten this morning. Master Edward and his dog never miss a meal."

Rathbourne paced behind his desk. "If this is one of his escapades, I'm going to… Lady Henrietta must not hear about this until we find him."

It was obvious that Rathbourne wasn't considering Edward's disappearance to be suspicious. Derrick couldn't ignore the possibility of a kidnapping. But certainly no one could have entered the house. The entire estate was guarded. And over half of the footmen were soldiers. But last night the household was in a state of total chaos—a perfect time for criminal action. But why a young boy? Leverage against Rathbourne and Kendal was a likely conclusion.

"When was the last time you saw Edward?" Ashworth, a close friend of the family, took over trying to calm the tutor's fright.

The awkward man swallowed hard. "Late last night. I waited downstairs for Mr. Brompton to check that Master Edward remained with the family. Brompton reassured me Edward was with the family, and that I could retire."

"How do you know Edward hasn't eaten?" Derrick asked, hoping this was all a misunderstanding due to the tired staff.

"Edward usually eats breakfast with Lady Rathbourne and his uncle, and then we meet in the small library to begin our studies. But, because of the late night, no one was in the breakfast room. I assumed he was still sleeping, so I waited in the library, preparing the lessons. When he didn't appear, I went to his room to check."

Rathbourne moved closer, staring at the young man. "What is it, Marlowe? What aren't you telling me?"

Derrick saw the young man flinch. The tutor's eyes darted to Rathbourne's face and then back to the floor.

"Go ahead, spit it out. Lord Rathbourne will not reprimand you if it helps find the young whelp," Ashworth said.

"Edward lately has been upset." Marlowe eyes remained focused on the rug.

"Upset?" Rathbourne barked. "And why haven't you shared this before now?"

Mr. Marlowe cleared his throat. "He never confided what was upsetting him, but I could tell he wasn't his usual spirited self. Edward hasn't been able to spend as much time with his family since the marriage of Lord Kendal, and Lady Rathbourne's condition." The young tutor's freckly face turned bright red with the mention of Lady Henrietta. Of course, Rathbourne glaring at the young man further undermined his confidence.

"Do you have any idea where Edward might have gone if he was upset?" Derrick asked.

"He and Gus love hiding in the woods. They can disappear there, making themselves impossible to find."

"That is very helpful, Marlowe," Ashworth added.

"I'm aware that Edward spends a lot of time with his uncle. Have you checked with Uncle Charles?" Derrick asked.

"Uncle Charles is still abed this morning. And I didn't want to alert Brompton to my concerns."

"Anything else? Anywhere else you've checked?" Derrick asked.

"I've gone through the house and into the stables..." Marlowe's voice cracked. "I'm sorry, Lord Rathbourne. I've failed in my duties."

Ashworth patted him on the shoulder. "You did well to come to Lord Rathbourne first."

"Lord Ashworth is correct. You did well, Marlowe. Return to the library and act as if nothing out of the ordinary has occurred. Do you understand? I do not want my wife to hear of this." Rathbourne turned his back, dismissing him.

The tutor scurried out of the room.

"I can understand your concern that Lady Henrietta not be told." Ash looked at Rathbourne. "But do you think it's wise not to inform the staff? Surely the Bromptons can be trusted not to inform her ladyship. And Edward might have confided in them."

Rathbourne walked to the large window and looked out at the downpour.

Derrick didn't want to be the one to raise the possibility of kidnapping.

"You're right, of course. I will speak to the Bromptons. And notify Kendal. He must know about his brother," Rathbourne said.

"We must consider foul play," Ashworth said.

"Yes, we must consider the possibility." Rathbourne ran his fingers through his hair.

"The chances are very unlikely, since it is impossible to infiltrate the estate. I will send a man to Kendal."

"I will question the guards on duty and inquire if there was any suspicious activity. I will also take men with me and start a search of the woods," Derrick said.

Rathbourne turned back to the room. His tiredness and the shared emotions of the birth must have contributed to his willingness to speak openly. "Henrietta will be devastated if anything has happened to the boy."

Derrick hoped to hell that Amelia remained occupied with the wedding and didn't visit Lady Henrietta today. After yesterday's cricket game with Edward, he had witnessed how close Amelia was to Edward, treating him like another younger brother.

"I need to talk with my aunt." Rathbourne strode to the door. "She and Edward have become close. She might have some insight into his disappearance. Once I've spoken to everyone, I'll join you in the search."

"I will report what I learn from the guards as soon as I've finished questioning them," Derrick added.

"I'll divide the estate into areas to be searched and assign the men between us," Ashworth said.

"We can each take an area," Rathbourne said over his shoulder as he rushed out of the room.

CHAPTER SIX

Edward drifted down the unlit path through Rathbourne's back garden. He knew every inch of the estate since he and Gus spent hours exploring the woods during the summer. The raindrops from the trees dripped down into his collar, and his boots sank in the muddy path from the recent downpour.

Gus followed reluctantly, probably because at this time of night, the yellow Labrador was usually comfortably asleep in front of the fire in Edward's bedroom. It had been easy to slip past the guards in the middle of the night, since he and Gus had observed their routine for months.

No one would notice until the afternoon hours that they were missing. Marlowe wouldn't look for him, since he'd assume Edward was sleeping in after the late night of celebration. And no one in his family would notice he was missing, since they were all wrapped up in the arrival of the new baby. What was so exciting about a baby who turned red in the face and hollered? Especially when everyone smiled and cooed like the next Earl of Rathbourne was a genius.

Edward trudged on, not sure of his destination, sure only that he must get away. He had no place at Rathbourne House. Nothing was the same since his siblings were married. He wished they could go back to when they had all lived together at Kendal House.

Now that Hen was going to be busy with her baby, it was time for him to leave. Many boys his age were already at Eton, as Michael had been. Hen hadn't wanted him to go last year after his ordeal of being kidnapped by a French spy. She pretended it was because she wanted him to get to know his new home, but for weeks after he was abducted, Hen would look at him and tear up. And Edward didn't want to leave Hen, or Michael, or Gus, or Uncle Charles, or the Bromptons.

He wanted to discuss Eton now, but since Michael's marriage to Gabby, Michael was always too busy. Gabby was swell, but Michael never had time for cricket or taking rides or playing chess. Uncle Charles still made time for him and Gus. But Uncle Charles was getting more forgetful and needed longer naps.

Edward fought the tears burning behind his eyelids—a man must not cry. And, at the age of twelve, he was almost a man. Why did his parents have to die, leaving him an orphan with no place where he belonged? He didn't have anyone except Gus.

Gus nudged Edward's hand with his wet nose. Edward knelt down on the soggy path, soaking his pants, but no one would notice or care if he got sick. Sniffling, he wrapped his arms around the stout chest of his loyal friend. Gus would never tell anyone about him acting like a namby-pamby. He didn't want to go to Eton and leave Gus behind—his pal, who was always ready for a game, a hike, a snack.

Gus licked Edward's face where the tears rolled down his cheeks. "Gus, I won't go to school unless they allow you to come with me. Cord is a very important person. And I bet he could make them accept you at Eton. You'd like all the boys. I'm sure they're fine chums. But we won't be able to raid the kitchen like we do at Rathbourne house." Edward wiped his nose on his jacket sleeve. "There are lots of rules, and neither of us is good at following the rules."

The moisture seeped into his pants, starting a chill. He stood and looked around the woods. They were close to the ravine that ran down to the river and the gamekeeper's hut. He didn't feel like slipping and sliding in the mud to the river tonight. "I'm getting hungry, and no one will be up to find out we raided the kitchen. Let's go."

Gus thumped his tail at the promise of food.

The dog suddenly froze in a rigid pose, his head stretched forward, his ears up and alert, his tail stiff and held high in the air. The dog's tense, still posture stirred the little hairs on Edward's neck.

Edward heard movement in the brush that must have alerted Gus. Not more than ten yards away from them on the main path, bushes were rustling.

Edward held his breath and listened carefully. Like Gus, he held himself tense and still. Because of the loud sound of the breaking branches and the movement of the brush across the path, Edward feared a large animal, maybe a wild boar, a lynx, or wolf was approaching.

Afraid to move, but more afraid Gus would try to attack the wild animal, Edward grabbed Gus's wet ruff. He said nothing to his dog in case the animal detected the sound. The noise stopped. Was the animal moving away? He and Gus stood frozen and waited.

And for the first time in his life, Gus didn't rush off and give chase, but stayed next to Edward in a protective stance, his ears perked up to every sound.

Edward also listened hard, leaning forward without moving

his feet, for fear of being discovered. Not a wild animal, but men speaking in French, if he heard correctly. Lucky for him, but too bad for the men, he was proficient in seven languages, including French. It was a family attribute.

A rough man's voice snarled. "It took you long enough."

"The family is up late."

"Lady Rathbourne had the baby, then?"

Edward's heart pounded hard and loud against his chest like a kettledrum. Convinced they could hear his thudding heart, he held his breath. He had to get closer to the conversation. Why were they discussing Hen? And Hen's baby? Could these men be French spies—French spies up to no good?

"It is time to put our plan in place. You will bring me the baby."

Edward almost gasped aloud, muffling his surprise at the last second with his hand.

"Monsieur, I beg you. Please spare my sister. I will do as you ask, as long as you promise to let her go."

These bastards were going to kidnap little Charles. Fear flooded Edward, causing his entire body to shake uncontrollably. The memory of his abduction rushed through him, making him want to run away as fast as he could.

He had to be brave. He had to find out who these men were, so Cord could stop the kidnapping. He couldn't let anything happen to Hen's baby. She was over the moon when he visited her—crying and laughing with the baby in her arms.

No, he couldn't run home like a ninny hammer. His brother and sister were English spies. And he was a Harcourt, and a Harcourt would never run from the French.

He dropped to his knees, ready to crawl. He pointed at Gus to stay. Gus with his wide, round body and protuberant belly, had little idea of stealth and no ability to move undetected.

Gus sat with his ears and head up and his body tense, recognizing this was no game of hide-and-seek. Gus was the one who found Edward after he was abducted and tied to a tree in the woods. If anything happened this time, Gus would rescue him again. Edward had no doubts about his dog's courage.

On all fours, his hands and knees sinking into the wet mud, he crawled slowly along the ravine toward the men. His heart pounded and reverberated in his ears. He held his breath as he carefully picked his way around the low-lying wild gooseberry and blueberry bushes.

"What did the English bitch have?"

"I beg you for mercy. Please, monsieur. You must have a sister. Please spare mine."

There was a rustle of sound. And Edward imagined the rough man twisting the other man's arm into submission. "Tell me. Is it a boy?"

Defeat filled the response. "Yes, monsieur. It is a boy."

"This is perfect." The man chuckled. "The minister will be pleased."

Edward's heart and mind sprinted. What French minister? Cord would know.

"In two nights, you and your sister will bring me the baby. Otherwise, your sister will suffer in ways you don't want to contemplate." He laughed like a maniac.

"Take me instead. Take me back to the prison, but spare my mother and sister."

Edward froze. Take him back to prison? Who at Rathbourne house had been in prison?

Edward creeped closer, aware of the ravine, straining for a

glimpse of the men through the trees. His sister and her baby were in danger. He had to expose the traitor at Rathbourne house.

"You and your sister will bring the baby to the hut. Or I will kill you both."

Edward slowly crept closer to the men who stood in a clearing in the woods.

"Did you hear a noise?"

Edward halted, his heart rushing like the river below him.

"You were followed. Someone is out there. Find him."

The fear of discovery made Edward startle abruptly. He couldn't stop the fall when his hands and knees slipped on the unstable, muddy slope.

CHAPTER SEVEN

Derrick rushed down the front steps to organize the search. The sun was breaking through the heavy clouds, and there was a lull in the rain. But for how long? Clearly a young boy wouldn't stay out all night in the rain as a prank, but he understood Cord's reasoning, based on Edward's history of shenanigans, to not jump to the conclusion that the disappearance indicated a subversive plot.

Derrick's queries with the staff unearthed no clues. The footmen and guards had remained at their posts through the night, and saw nothing suspicious.

As he headed to the stables to continue his questioning, a familiar coach arrived in front of the estate.

Of all the blasted luck. If he hadn't spent the time interviewing the staff, he could have avoided Amelia. He cursed upside and down under his breath. Tomorrow was her wedding day. Didn't she have wedding details to attend to? She should be enjoying all the folderol attendant on a wedding, not being involved with tracking down a missing boy. She was already exhausted from worrying about her friend's birth, and she didn't need the added stress of Edward's disappearance.

Derrick descended to assist his beloved, who peered out the window at him, down from the carriage. She was already smiling widely on seeing him. Dressed in a bright purple dress that clung to all her curves, with a sassy purple hat perched on the side of her head, she totally looked her part as a young, beautiful society woman free of cares. "Darling, where are you off to with such a scowl?"

Her eyes were bright and her voice cheerful—unlike him, she didn't show the strain from yesterday's long hours. He took her hand and pressed a kiss to her knuckles. Her eyes were shining with love, and he felt like a clod to regret seeing her.

"Lady Henrietta hasn't awoken yet. You should return later."

The light in Amelia's eyes dimmed with his curt tone.

And to make matters worse, Pierpont climbed out of the carriage after Amelia. The greasy Frenchman with his pomaded blond hair did his usual perusal of Derrick's dark morning coat and tan riding breeches. His thick lips puckered in disapproval. Did the flamboyant man know his name translated to "under the bridge." Not a fitting name for a man who prided himself on his own importance.

"I have no intention of bothering Hen," Amelia said quietly.

"Of course not. I wasn't… Then why are you not at home resting?"

"Pierpont and I are here to meet with the Rathbourne gardener. I'm sure I told you we are using flowers from both our hothouse and the Rathbournes', since I want the ballroom to be overflowing with lovely, fragrant bouquets."

He heard Pisspot's disapproving *tut* behind him. Derrick turned and glared at the thin, wiry man. Besides, he didn't like having the Frenchman behind him and out of sight. For a brief second, Derrick glimpsed a veiled, hostile look before Pierpont reverted to his usual exaggerated dandy manner, straightening his morning coat with his pinkies outthrust. Everything about the man put Derrick on edge.

"Pierpont, you may go ahead. I will escort Miss Bonnington." Derrick didn't want Pierpont listening to every word of his conversation with Amelia.

Pierpont raised his painted eyebrows before climbing the stairs to where a footman held the door open.

Derrick smiled down at his lovely bride, whose eyes had narrowed on his face. "I'm sorry I forgot about the flowers and your plans for today."

"You have far more important matters to worry about than flowers." Although she sounded like the usual animated Amelia, she didn't return his smile.

Derrick didn't know how to respond to Amelia's lack of sunny enthusiasm. It was so rare. And how was he lucky enough to attract such an amiable bride when he was known for his surly ways? He offered her his arm to escort her up the stairs.

"What is wrong, Derrick? Something is amiss."

Derrick struggled with how much to tell Amelia, knowing how deeply she cared for Edward, and how distressed she would become. But if he kept Edward's disappearance from her, she would be hurt and furious.

She stopped abruptly in the massive entranceway. "Derrick, what is it?"

"I must talk with you." Derrick nodded to the footman, and then guided Amelia to a side room while searching for the right words to lessen the shock.

"Now you're scaring me." Amelia's voice quivered.

He wanted to take her into his arms and reassure her. He wished he didn't have to deliver the news that would shatter her cheerful mood.

Amelia released his arm and turned toward him. "Is Henrietta ill? Is it Charles?"

He closed the door behind him. "Lady Henrietta is quite well, as is little Charles."

She inspected his face, staring into his eyes. "You're changing your mind about the wedding?"

"What? Of all the idiotic ideas!" He didn't mean to sound so sharp, but honestly, how could she even consider such a ridiculous possibility? "Of course not. Why would you think such a crazy thing?"

Amelia searched his face. "Because you're behaving as if doomsday has arrived, gloomy and downright menacing."

"Don't you know how much I love you?" he shouted.

A bright smile replaced her pinched lips. She rushed to him and threw her arms around him, pressing against him. "I was afraid you decided to not marry and have babies with me, after how awful it was last night. It was frightening enough to make a man rethink marriage."

This wasn't the time to discuss that after a sleepless night he had decided that they should wait to have children. He knew methods for preventing pregnancy. Although Amelia shone with happiness holding the tiny baby in her arms, she wasn't ready for pregnancy. If he was honest, he wasn't ready either.

He tightened his hold on her. He could never chance losing her. She was his light, shining just for him.

He tweaked her pert nose. "You might regret marrying me once you find out that I snore."

"Do you snore?" The teasing lilt in her voice forced him to steal a kiss from her soft, beckoning lips.

"I might."

She kissed him back unreservedly, opening her mouth to him, and he accepted the irresistible invitation. His tongue savored the sweet flavor of Amelia. He wanted more than a taste. Her soft breasts crushed against him, and her little gasps of breath weren't helping his resolve. He had to stop before getting started.

He released his hold. "Darling, I do have upsetting news. It might be better if you sit down." He took her arm and led her to the settee.

Amelia pulled away. "Derrick, I'm not the type of woman to faint. Please tell me. This mysterious manner of yours is frightening me."

"Edward has gone missing."

She shook her head. "Pish-posh. Edward is up to his usual antics. If I know Edward, he was up early, and when no one was about, he decided to go off on an adventure without Mr. Marlowe. Edward becomes bored very easily."

She knew Edward well, as demonstrated yesterday during the cricket practice—Amelia bossed and mothered him exactly as she did her younger brothers.

She straightened her hat, which had been knocked askew by his embrace. "That is the news that has you treating me gingerly, like a frail flower?" Amelia laughed.

Derrick wished he didn't have to upset Amelia. "I'm hoping you're right. But his bed wasn't slept in, and he and Gus missed breakfast."

"His bed wasn't slept in?" Amelia paced in the small waiting room. "Edward and Gus never miss a meal."

Amelia stopped at the window overlooking the front of the estate. "Has Cord or Michael searched for him?"

"We've sent a message to Kendal, and when I saw your

coach, I was on my way to the stables to gather the men for the search."

When he saw her concern, his resolution to leave her behind weakened.

"I must come with you."

Derrick had prepared himself for Amelia's demand, but he still had to try to prevent her from participating in a wet, muddy search that might end up with a disastrous outcome.

"How far do you think you can go dressed in that gown? The paths and woods will be muddy. And you wouldn't want to slow the men down."

Amelia's light eyes flashed. He had only seen that heated look when she was in her competitive, I-will-win mode of playing cricket.

"I'll wear my cricket dress. I have one here in case of an impromptu game. Must I remind you that I'm very fit, and will not be the one to slow the men down?"

Derrick hadn't considered that Amelia's special dress was at Rathbourne House. The outfit was designed like pantaloons, giving her fast and easy movement, in addition to hugging her irresistible derriere.

His jaw tightened in frustration. She was going to go parade herself in front of all the guards. He didn't like to think of himself as possessive, but when it came to Amelia, he couldn't seem to stifle his primitive instincts. "What if it rains? You'll get soaking wet right before our wedding. You don't want to be ill."

"Of all the asinine arguments." She flung her arms into the air. "Edward is missing."

"Are you suggesting my concern for you and your health is asinine?"

"I didn't mean it that way." She tried to suppress the smile tugging on the corners of her mouth. "Well, kind of." Amelia's eyes danced in amusement, and he was bewitched. He was going to lose a lot of arguments with his appealing wife-to-be, and the idea didn't unsettle him in the least.

"Derrick, be reasonable. You must see that finding Edward has to be the priority. If anything happened to him… Oh, bollocks. You haven't told Hen, have you? We must keep it from her. I'll speak to Mrs. Brompton."

"Cord has already spoken to the Bromptons. No one plans to inform Lady Henrietta until after we find Edward."

"We need to contact Gwyneth. She'll know all the best hiding places on the estate." Amelia paced back and forth like a colt confined to its pen. "You're not suspecting a French threat, are you? You haven't forgotten that Edward was abducted by the French to force Hen to surrender a code book."

He respected Amelia's reasoning. It would be easy to misjudge her intelligence because of her obsession with fashion and art. "Not yet. We're all treating it as a possible prank." He didn't include a prank that had possibly gone wrong, very wrong.

The color washed out of Amelia's face. "Why would the French want Edward? He is only a boy."

Derrick chose not to mention that he was the brother of England's top code breakers.

Amelia took a deep breath. "I'm going upstairs to change my clothes. I'll meet you at the stable to begin the search with the men. I refuse to not help. Edward trusts me, and I must find him for Hen. She would absolutely do the same if Colin or Drew were missing."

He pulled her back into his arms. "I had hoped to talk you out of this, but I understand. I wouldn't be able to wait either. You must promise me you will stay by my side. And if I perceive there is danger, you'll listen to me."

"But what kind of danger could we possibly confront on the Rathbourne estate?"

He tipped her chin up with one finger and stared into her eyes. "Promise me."

CHAPTER EIGHT

Amelia trudged through the mud positioned between Derrick and an oversized man she had never before seen on Rathbourne estate. The red, puckered scar across his cheek spoke of a military past, so he must be one of the many unseen guards who were on the grounds watching for intruders.

A youth, as burly as the other guard, walked ahead, his rifle at the ready.

A feeling of panic enveloped her. Men with rifles searching for sweet Edward. How could this day of promise have turned so quickly into a disaster?

It was not how she imagined she'd spend the day before her wedding. Her preoccupation with every detail—such as whether the shade of the roses matched the table covering and ballroom wall fabric—had become insignificant, overshadowed by her worry for Edward.

She and the men took turns shouting for Edward and Gus. Except to shout Edward's name, Derrick had remained silent since she proposed they look for the boy at the gamekeeper's hut.

After all his resistance to her participation, she couldn't believe how readily he agreed to her suggestion. A man of few words, like her father, Derrick had responded by saying only, "Makes sense."

When she arrived at the stables, Derrick had inspected her from her hair pulled up into a topknot to her half boots. The way his gaze lingered on her thighs had brought a burn to her cheeks and butterflies to her stomach. And the way he glared at the men accompanying them was downright embarrassing. Her cricket dress covered more than any dress a lady of fashion wore.

And though she was already wearing a cloak, he took off his and wrapped it around her while whispering, "Only I get to stare at your sweet bottom." When he tied the cord around her throat, he promised, "And tomorrow night, I plan to do more than stare."

She looked up at the man who walked next to her silently, his jutting, hard jaw speckled with unshaven stubble. This striking man could make her heart riot with one glance. He obviously hadn't taken the time to shave this morning, and she wanted to rub her hand along the dark bristles, kiss the tender skin along his pale throat, and kiss down his wide, muscular chest.

Derrick felt her gaze. He looked down, his black eyes probing hers.

Heat immediately shot to her face at being caught daydreaming about her handsome, rugged husband-to-be.

Derrick's eyes darkened while he watched the blush spread across her face. He grinned, his perfect white teeth gleaming. The blasted man rarely smiled, but was now reading her mind and enjoying her embarrassment.

Well, two could play the game. Taking a very long time, she slowly licked her lips, and enjoyed watching his body tighten before he took an audible breath.

He bent close and whispered, "You're playing a very dangerous game."

Pleasurable expectation for her wedding night surged through her until one of the men startled her with his shout of Edward's name. How could she have so easily forgotten the reason for their presence in the woods?

Guilty for her moment of distraction, she shouted, her voice pinching in desperation. "Edward! Gus!"

Derrick took her arm and tugged her close to his side. "Not how I wanted you to spend the day before our wedding. We're going to find him. I promise."

Amelia appreciated Derrick's assurance. If there was any man strong and smart enough to find Edward, it was Derrick. But what if the French had taken Edward away from the estate?

"How much farther to the gamekeeper's hut?" Derrick asked.

She released her breath and focused on the task ahead. "If I'm not mistaken, it is right around the corner. The hut is at the river's edge, and there is a narrow path along the ravine to take us down there."

She wasn't definite about the exact turn in the trail. When she had come with the boys, there were no somber men with guns, no threat of the French, only play, frolicking, and enjoyment. But now…her heart drummed a thunderous beat, and fear lodged in her throat.

Hours before she was worried that the cut of her ball gown was too bold for a new bride. Now it seemed silly. Was she a shallow woman after all, like the many society women who only cared about their pleasure and their appearances?

Her brothers and her father teased her relentlessly, first about her art, then when she began to sketch fashions. No one understood that creating was the only part of her life she could control. When her mother died and she was left responsible for her brothers, she used her art to assuage her pain. Her art was a refuge which allowed her to put on a brave face for her father and her younger brothers when they looked to her for comfort. She had always reassured all of them, but now she questioned whether she had the strength or the courage to comfort Hen if they didn't find Edward. Her fear fed her resolve. She wouldn't stop until they found the boy.

"How do you know these woods so well?"

"Edward, Colin, Drew, and I have spent many hours in these woods."

"You brought the boys out here by yourself?"

"Mr. Marlowe would accompany me. We would explore for hours in the hopes of tiring the boys. But it was always Mr. Marlowe and I who ended up exhausted after our outing." She shouted again, trying to quash her panicky feelings. "Edward! Gus!"

Suddenly they all stopped at the faint sound of a wild, insistent bark.

"Gus." Amelia shouted again. Her mind raced to why Edward's dog was responding but not Edward. The dog started a round of urgent howls.

Amelia was about to roar when Derrick covered her mouth with his hand. He shook his head and whispered. "It might be a trap."

A trap? The French were using Gus to lure them farther into the woods—to the ravine? Her heart bumped loudly in her ears.

"Stay here." He nodded to the man next to Amelia, who pointed his rifle toward the sound of Gus.

Silently, Derrick waved to the young man to circle to the right while he walked into the woods, directly toward the sound. But if it was a trap, Derrick would be the target. Now her heart sped out of control like a curricle race gone bad.

She held still, taking care not to risk Derrick's safety.

But Gus's bark had sounded like a cry for help. If someone held Edward, Gus would be snarling and barking crazily. She wanted to share this thought with Derrick, who, with his gun pointed into the woods, walked carefully and quietly ahead.

Gus now barked frantically, yipping in a high-pitched howl, apparently set off by Derrick's approach.

She turned toward the nearby guard and whispered. "Gus is calling for help. Can't you tell?"

"I can't say, m'lady."

It took all of Amelia's self-control not to run after Derrick, but, keeping her promise, she restrained herself.

"Amelia, I've found him," Derrick yelled.

CHAPTER NINE

Amelia rushed toward the sound of Derrick's voice, her heart and stomach performing somersaults.

Derrick yelled again from a spot deep within the woods, "Over here, Amelia."

When she finally cleared the scrub, she skirted around the trees. Ten feet ahead, Derrick was on his stomach, leaning over the edge of the ravine with his arm extended. Gus was lying down too, peering over the edge, keening a desperate noise.

"You can do it, old man. Gus is waiting for you."

Amelia couldn't muster a breath, and the backs of her knees tingled. Edward had fallen down a steep incline that dropped fifty feet to the river.

Derrick spoke in a calm, reassuring voice, without looking up. "Amelia's here now, Edward. We're going to take you home."

"I want Amelia." Edward's plaintive cry had Amelia jumping over the last bushes to get close to the edge.

"Edward, I'm here." She peeked over the lip of the cliff. Edward was perched on a rocky outcropping five feet down, the width of a small table. One false move and he would plummet down to the river.

Icy shivers ran up and down her spine. Derrick leaned farther out over the muddy hillside while the young soldier held his ankles to secure him. The soft, muddy earth where she stood wasn't solid or stable.

Derrick was a very heavy man, at least sixteen stone.

The weight of two large men could make the soft cliff easily give way.

Derrick spoke evenly to Edward. "I want you to get to your knees very carefully. Since your ankle is hurt, you will be more secure if you kneel rather than try to stand."

Amelia covered her mouth to suppress a gasp. If Edward stood up…

"Edward, do as Derrick says. Get to your knees. Slowly, now." Amelia tried to sound as calm as Derrick.

Edward's face was ashen, and his eyes were wide with terror.

"Any snack you want for you and Gus once we get home. I promise."

"Gus and I have been here all night. I thought…" His sob broke off.

Amelia, realizing she had crept too close to the edge, quickly flattened herself to the ground. "We're going to take you home and pamper you like a prince. That's it, nice and slow, to your knees."

Rocks from the cliff crashed over the side, echoing in the silent woods as Edward extended his arms. He flinched, but completed the move from sitting to kneeling.

"Come on Edward, almost there," Derrick coaxed. "Now, slowly reach up with your hand, and I will pull you the rest of the way."

Edward stared down, following the path of the falling rocks that skittered down when he shifted his position.

Derrick commanded, "Don't look down. You need to give me your hand."

"Darling, please give Derrick your hand. He is very strong, and will be able to lift you, I promise. And the sooner you do, the sooner we can be on our way home to a fire and food and dry clothes."

Edward tentatively inched his hand upward toward Derrick's outstretched arm. Derrick wrapped his strong, broad hand around Edward's wrist. "Here you go." In one, smooth move, Derrick pulled Edward into the arms of the soldier who waited at the edge.

Gus immediately jumped on the soldier's leg, trying to reach Edward.

"Gus wouldn't leave. I told him to go, but he stayed." Edward sniffed.

Derrick stood carefully, and then reached for Amelia to pull her to her feet. "I want to get all of us off this blasted, sodden cliff." He took Amelia's arm and followed the soldier carrying Edward. A yelping Gus tagged along, right next to Edward.

Edward peeked around the younger man. "I want Derrick to carry me."

Amelia took off Derrick's cloak and wrapped it around Edward.

Derrick smiled. "Guess you know who is the strongest." He winked at the young man, who was quite capable of carrying Edward.

In the transfer, Edward cried out in pain.

Amelia gasped. "What is it, Edward? Are you hurt?"

Derrick said, "He twisted his ankle. We will take a good look at the ankle when we get back. Anything else bothering you?"

"Yes, I'm cold and hungry. Any chance you brought snacks for Gus and me, Amelia?"

Amelia mentally chastised herself for not thinking to bring food and a blanket.

Hearing Edward's plea reassured Amelia that the young boy and his dog were already recovering from the scare, far more quickly than the adults who had been searching for them.

Amelia took off her cloak and laid the wool across the front of Edward. "You're chilled, but we will soon have you warmed up."

Derrick raised his eyebrows, but chose not to say anything about her cricket dress.

CHAPTER TEN

Derrick strode quickly down the path, forcing Amelia to speed her pace to keep up. He wanted to get Edward back to the house. He pulled the boy's slight frame closer against his chest, hoping his heat would start to warm him. The boy had spent all night out in the wet and cold. Edward's relief at being rescued would quickly fade, and Derrick knew from personal experience that the physical and emotional trauma would soon catch up.

Amelia hurried to pat the boy's arm. "Are you starting to warm up, Edward?"

Edward shivered again. "I'm cold, but not wet, since the cliff protected me from the rain. But Gus was in the rain all night."

"Well it's lucky that Gus has a warm winter coat." Amelia squeezed his arm, and tried to look calm. "Edward, why did you go out by yourself in the middle of the night? Were you upset about something?"

"It isn't important now. I must speak with Cord right away."

"First we must get you warmed up and find you something to eat."

"I must talk to Cord first."

"He is out searching for you," Derrick said.

Edward swallowed hard. "Blasted, Cord must not be happy to have to search for me when he has other important matters to attend to."

Derrick refrained from commenting on the important matters, including trying to prevent France's invasion of England.

Edward sagged against Derrick. "Oh, I hope Aunt Euphemia isn't looking for me, too." Derrick understood Edward's trepidation. Aunt Euphemia intimidated grown men.

"No one will be upset with you," Amelia crooned. "Everyone is going to be happy that you're well."

A shout echoed in the woods. "Brinsley, where are you?"

Gus barked at the familiar voice.

Kendal came tearing around the bend in the path "Thank God. When I heard Gus's bark…" His eyes filled and his voice cracked. "Thank God." Kendal rushed toward Edward. "Where have you been? Are you injured?"

"I twisted my ankle. And I fell partway down a cliff," Edward replied matter-of-factly, as if falling off a cliff was a routine experience.

"You fell off a cliff?" Kendal bellowed.

Whether it was the sight of his brother or Kendal's roar, Edward started to cry. "I was so afraid no one would find Gus and me."

Kendal lifted the boy out of Derrick's arms, his face rigid with suppressed feelings. "I would keep searching until I found you." He hugged his brother tight. "If anything had happened to you…" Kendal exhaled loudly. "But why in blazes were you out by yourself in the middle of the night?"

Amelia's eyes clouded with tears. Derrick took her arm and pulled her next to his side. She wrapped her arm around his waist, snuggling closer for his warmth. They had been out for hours. She whispered, "Thank you for finding him and pulling him off the cliff."

"At your service, my lady." He wrapped his arm around her shoulder, wanting her closer. She was a loving, gentle woman who, after tomorrow, would be his.

Amelia walked next to Kendal with Derrick on the outside.

"I have something important to tell you," Edward insisted.

"Not as important as what I have to say to you, young man. If you ever pull a stunt like this again, I'm going to blister your backside."

Edward giggled, not in the least intimidated by his brother's threat.

Amelia had told Derrick that as a youth Kendal was constantly in trouble for his escapades. No wonder Edward wasn't afraid.

Derrick didn't want to think about his father's response when he fell into boyish pranks. His oldest brother bore the brunt of their father's wrath, since he was the heir, and his brother had followed his father's lead, and resorted to alcohol and violence as the ultimate answer to any problem. Since meeting Amelia, Derrick began to believe he wasn't destined to follow in his father and brother's footsteps. Amelia's love and faith in him had changed him for the better.

Kendal playfully shook Edward in his arms. "You have the nerve to laugh. I might have to send you to the black chamber."

"As if there is one in England," Edward challenged.

"The black chamber?" Derrick asked.

Edward leaned around Amelia to see Derrick. "In the reign of Louis XIV, the cryptographers were held in the basement of Versailles. Louis had a very large network of spies and code breakers. He was very good at the spy business."

"I still think it's the black chamber for you and Gus," Kendal teased.

Gus yelped at the mention of his name.

"Michael, you have to listen. I heard two Frenchmen planning to kidnap Hen's baby."

Amelia felt as if she could barely pull air into her lungs. "The baby? They want to take Hen's baby?"

Derrick tightened his hold on her shoulders before he realized he might be hurting her.

Kendal stopped and looked down at his brother. "Is this one of your stories to save yourself from punishment?"

"No, I would never make up a story to hurt Hen or Charles. You need to believe me. They plan to abduct the baby tomorrow night. The younger man is to bring Charles to the gamekeeper's hut or the bad man will harm his sister."

Derrick's brain battled with the possibility. Edward had gone through a trauma. Had he really heard Frenchmen on the estate plotting to kidnap Rathbourne's heir? Tomorrow night was the wedding ball at Bonnington estate. Everyone would be away from the Rathbourne estate to attend the ball.

"Were they in the woods? Is that where you heard them?" Derrick tried to gentle his tone.

How had the French gotten on the Rathbourne estate? His men were guarding the borders, but the estate spanned acres, making it difficult to patrol the expansive area.

"Gus and I were by the ravine. We hid in the woods when we heard them coming. I was crawling closer to get a better view of the men's faces when I fell off the cliff."

Amelia cried out. "Edward, you could have…" Derrick felt her tremors of fear against his side. The last twenty-four hours had been a nightmare for Amelia. How could she handle any more stress? She should be excited and immersed in all the wedding folderol she had been working on for months, not facing a threat looming over her friend's baby.

Derrick's muscles clenched, ready for action, ready to terminate and decimate anyone willing to harm an innocent infant and destroy his beloved's happiness on the eve of her wedding. Kidnapping an infant had the dark and sinister mark of that foul mastermind, Fouche.

Kendal was focused on his brother's ashen face. "Go on. Tell me the rest."

"When the rough older man said he heard something, they started to search for me. I could hear them getting closer, and that was when I panicked and lost my footing." Edward's voice quivered. "And the ground gave out, and I fell through space. I thought…"

Kendal rubbed his brother's hair. "You're safe now."

"I must have hit my head. The next thing I knew I was lying on the ledge with Gus looking down at me from above, and the men were gone."

Gus whined and jumped on Kendal's leg, trying to reach Edward, reacting to the distress in Edward's voice.

Amelia pulled out of Derrick's embrace and took Edward's hand. "Dearest, it's finished now. You don't have to worry anymore. Derrick, Michael, and Cord will stop these men. Let's get you home, and then you can tell them all the details after you've gotten warm and rested."

Amelia gave both men a look signaling a halt to any further questions.

Kendal nodded to Amelia in understanding. "You're safe now. Think about what a story you'll be able to tell the Bromptons and Uncle Charles about falling off a cliff. But not a word to our sister, do you understand? Not a word to Hen. And definitely not a word about the kidnapping."

Edward nodded and then wiped his nose on Derrick's cloak.

"My back and arms are giving out." Kendal pretended to drop Edward. "You and Gus have been eating too many of Bromie's biscuits."

Edward snickered.

Amelia sniffled and dabbed at her wet cheeks.

"Not strong enough to carry the boy, Kendal?" Derrick joked, shifting the attention away from Amelia's tears.

Amelia wrapped her arm around Derrick's waist and mouthed a silent "thank you."

Kendal's eyes gleamed. "Edward, did you know that Brinsley stood behind a tree to guard my house in Paris for weeks?"

Derrick feigned an aggrieved tone. "Do you know how cold and wet I was while standing in the woods watching your brother?"

Edward looked up in awe at Derrick. "How big was the tree?"

Derrick chuckled. "A very big and very old tree."

"You were in Paris to protect Michael?"

Derrick was about to respond, but Kendal beat him.

Kendal shook his head. "He was assigned to spy on me."

Edward watched each man's face while the two bantered.

"My assignment was to keep you safe."

Amelia took Derrick's hand, acknowledging his past jealousy of Kendal. When he met Amelia, she believed herself in love with Kendal because of their childhood friendship. It was true, he had been jealous of Kendal's closeness to Amelia. But that was months ago. Kendal was smitten with his talented wife. And Amelia was his. Was she worried that the joking between the men was more than a game to distract Edward?

"And look how that worked out. I was shot." Kendal was enjoying himself too much at Derrick's expense.

"In your arse!" Edward snorted.

"Did you know that your brother dressed up as a nun to escape Paris?" Derrick asked innocently. "He wore a white dress and an enormous, strange hat on his head."

Derrick didn't like reliving the memory of when his charge, Kendal, left the house dressed as a nun and pranced up to Fouche's dangerous and unpredictable Black Guards. But he had to give Kendal credit. It was a bold, brave act. And it worked. Kendal had escaped Paris.

"Yes, he told me and Hen all about his adventure in France. I wish I could have seen it. Gabby tells me he made a pretty and convincing nun."

Kendal again shook Edward in his arms. "My wife would never say such an outrageous thing!"

Edward started laughing. "You were there when she said you were a pretty nun."

Kendal huffed in feigned outrage. "Remind me to cut her clothing budget."

Derrick added, "Maybe we can have a masquerade ball, and your brother can dress up again for all of London to see."

Edward howled.

Not wanting to be left out, Gus jumped on Kendal again.

Kendal winked at Derrick.

When they approached the road leading to Rathbourne house, Amelia pointed ahead to the dark, turreted Jacobean residence. "We're almost home, Edward. I'm sure Mrs. Brompton has something special for you, and treats for Gus."

Gus barked at the mention of treats.

"Gus recognizes that word. I've been teaching him t-r-e-a-t-s in seven languages. I think he's caught on to the spelling too, although he still responds the most to English. Most likely since English is his first language."

Derrick chuckled. Amelia had told him about Edward's prodigious skills with language, mathematics, and codes, but he hadn't spent much time with the lad, except on the cricket field. And during the fierce competition, one spoke only to encourage one's teammates.

"Oh, I'm in for it. Look at that scowl on Cord's face," Edward said.

Amelia waved at Rathbourne, who stood on the front steps, his legs spread as if braced for battle. "He isn't angry with you, Edward. He was worried," Amelia reassured.

Derrick wasn't as convinced about Rathbourne's understanding nature when it came to boyish antics that caused stress to his wife. But Derrick knew Amelia wouldn't allow Rathbourne to hurt the boy's feelings.

They made their way to the front of the estate, where several guards were positioned.

Rathbourne rushed down the stairs. "Thank God you're safe. You better have a darn good reason for this latest infraction."

"I'm sorry for the worry, but you'll be glad that I was missing."

"How can I possibly be happy that you were missing?" Rathbourne ran his hand over his hair. "Only a Harcourt could say something as nonsensical and convoluted."

"Careful, old man," Kendal warned. "Edward has important news, but I think we should take him into the library and away from listening ears."

Rathbourne looked to Derrick, who nodded.

Amelia took Rathbourne's arm as they climbed the stairs. "You must remember that Edward is only the messenger for this most difficult news."

Rathbourne glared at Amelia as if she had lost her mind. Derrick waited for Rathbourne's reaction, ready to defend Amelia from any censure.

"I'm sure I'm capable of refraining from blaming Edward for whatever news he plans to share."

Amelia and Rathbourne followed Kendal and Edward into the library. "Michael, move him close to the fire." Amelia directed. "I'm going to find the Bromptons. We must send for a doctor to examine Edward's injuries."

"Injuries? I thought he was tired."

"Edward will explain everything, but he twisted his ankle."

Amelia paused, taking Edward's hand. "These men will handle the spies. You must not worry about anything but getting better."

Then Amelia addressed Rathbourne before bustling to the door. "You'll be grateful for Edward's information."

She smiled at Derrick as she hurried out of the room.

Rathbourne blew out a loud breath. "Will someone tell me what the hell is going on?"

Kendal walked to the fireplace and stood with his back to Rathbourne. "Go ahead and tell him."

Rathbourne moved next to Edward. "I'm waiting."

Edward gulped, then blurted out. "I overheard French spies in the woods last night plotting to kidnap Charles tomorrow night."

Derrick wasn't sure how Rathbourne would react, but he knew what he would do if anyone threatened Amelia.

Rathbourne stiffened and fisted his hands at his side. "Go on, tell me everything."

Edward, now confident that he wouldn't be on the receiving end of Rathbourne's wrath, recounted everything he overheard, in detail.

The only visible sign of Rathbourne's reaction was the slight, barely noticeable tic in his thick jaw.

"You were very brave to try to see the men's faces. I'm thankful you are not badly injured. I'm not sure what story we will tell your sister, but she must not know about the threat against Charles. Do you understand?"

"Edward understands that Hen needs rest, and that she must not experience any stress. Isn't that so?" Kendal said, looking at his brother.

"I'd never do anything to worry Hen."

Derrick waited to see how Rathbourne would respond to the boy's ignorance of how traumatic his disappearance would be for his sister.

Rathbourne rubbed Edward's hair. "You did well."

"I didn't see the man's face, but I could identify his voice," Edward added.

"You are not to be involved. Do you understand?" Rathbourne didn't raise his voice, but by the harsh tone, he left no doubt that this was a command.

"Kendal, take him up the back stairwell, away from Henrietta's rooms, to Gwyneth's old drawing room."

Kendal nodded. "I will stay with Edward until the doctor arrives, but I'll want to be apprised of the plans."

Derrick rushed to open the door. The toll of retelling his torment was etched in Edward's ashen face and the way he lay listless in Kendal's arms.

"I thank you, my lord, for rescuing me off the cliff."

Derrick nodded. "It was no problem. You know, you're much easier to watch over than your brother."

But Edward had closed his eyes, already asleep in his brother's arms.

Kendal, needing to have the last word, whispered, "You're never going forget Paris, are you?"

Derrick rubbed his chin. "Most likely not."

CHAPTER ELEVEN

Derrick closed the door and sat in his chair across from Rathbourne's desk, watching his superior pace in front of the window.

A knife-sharp tension permeated the cavernous room.

Shoulders rigid, jaw jutted, clenching and unclenching his fists—Rathbourne was in a silent, burning rage. Derrick imagined Rathbourne was mentally choking the life out of the men who dared to threaten his newborn infant.

Derrick said nothing. What could he add to the fury the men were experiencing? They all had killed men in their line of work. And at times the killing lines got blurred, but never would any man of honor harm an infant. Fouche would burn in hell for his evil, and Derrick wanted to help send him on his way.

Rathbourne turned. "I want Ash to handle this newest threat. He should be back soon from the search. I sent word to the men when you returned with Edward."

Derrick sat forward. "I want to be part of taking these bastards down."

Rathbourne tunneled his fingers through his hair. "No, you are the bridegroom. The wedding must go on as planned, so we don't alert them that we're aware of their plan. Besides,

Henrietta would have my hide if I interfered with Amelia's wedding."

And as if both men didn't immediately think of his wife's reaction if anything happened to her babe, Rathbourne strode back to the window and stared out at the grounds.

"What is taking Ash so damn long?"

Grateful for action, Derrick jumped up. "I'll check whether he's returned. Since he doesn't know of this latest threat, he might not hurry."

Rathbourne nodded. Not changing his brooding stance.

Too impatient to wait for the footman, Derrick opened the door. Pierpont stepped back when the door flew open.

Derrick surged forward, crowding the Frenchman.

"Why are you in this hall, Pierpont?" There was no need for Pierpont to be in the family quarters.

Pierpont didn't flinch at Derrick's intimidating posture. Pierpont definitely had balls. Most men would have given Derrick space, well aware of the damage he could inflict.

Pierpont patted his pomaded hair and spoke in his usual, irritating sing-song voice.

"I thought I heard Mademoiselle Amelia's voice. She's been gone for hours, and she needs to make some important decisions."

Derrick watched the Frenchman's eyes shift to the open door of the library. Had he been lurking in the hall when they returned with Edward? Where was the footman-guard who was always stationed at the door? He had been there when they arrived. Most likely he was now assisting Kendal and Amelia getting Edward settled.

Despite Amelia's trust in her protégé, Derrick did not share her favorable opinion. He wanted Pisspot away from Amelia, away from Rathbourne House, and away from England. If he had his way, he would banish the snake back to France.

"Miss Amelia has left word that you should return to Bonnington Estate."

"But what about the flower arrangements?"

Derrick inched closer to make sure Pierpont felt the difference in their size and strength, and recognized who would win in a battle between them.

"You are to make those decisions, but Miss Amelia wants you back at Bonnington House. She says there are important details you must see to."

Pierpont's lower lip curled before he executed a formal bow. "As you wish, my lord."

Was Derrick imagining the insolence in his response? Derrick waited and watched Pierpont saunter down the hallway, his hips swaying in an overly affected manner, as if he knew Derrick was watching. It was impossible not to suspect everyone, including an inconsequential designer, when treachery threatened.

Derrick didn't have time to sort out the mystery surrounding the French designer when there was a real threat against Cord's family.

Derrick moved toward the door when Ashworth came striding down the hall.

"What the hell, Brinsley? Scowl much?" Ash slapped him on the back. "For a man who is about to marry, you don't look as if the prospect of wedded bliss is agreeing with you."

Derrick shook his head.

"Is something wrong with Edward? Or Charles?"

"For now they are both fine."

"God, Brinsley your cryptic comments…"

Derrick leaned down to Ashworth and said in a quiet voice, "Not here. In the library. Rathbourne is waiting for us."

Ashworth hastened his steps.

Rathbourne turned at the men's entrance.

"What the hell, Cord? You're spending too much time with Brinsley. You're starting to glower in precisely the same manner."

Ashworth's joke fell flat when both men glared at him.

He threw up his hands. "Forgive me. I thought that you two would at least crack a smile after finding Edward." Ashworth walked to the brandy table. "You look like you both need a drink. And if you don't, I do. What a blasted, muddy mess."

Brompton, at almost a run, dashed in the room before the footman could close the door. Breathless, he paused. "Excuse me, my lord. I wouldn't interrupt if it weren't important."

"Lady Henrietta?" Rathbourne rushed toward Brompton.

"No, my lord. Her ladyship and babe are fine. But it is about his little lordship."

Rathbourne growled. "What about Charles?"

Brompton's voice quivered. "It is very irregular, but Lisette, the new French maid, and her brother have requested an immediate audience with you. I explained I would handle whatever problem they were having with adjusting to the household. But they insist it has nothing to do with their duties, but that…"

Ashworth threw back a taste, and then walked over to the elder butler, who had frozen. "Brompton, whatever you have to say will not upset his lordship. He appreciates what an outstanding job you and your wife do."

"Thank you, Lord Ashworth. In all my years, I have never

had to handle anything this upsetting, despite the extreme irregularities at Harcourt House. I am flummoxed as to how to proceed. I…"

Derrick interrupted before Rathbourne could explode. "What do they want to tell Lord Rathbourne about the baby?"

Brompton whispered, "That they were sent from France to kidnap the baby."

Ashworth choked on the brandy. "Bloody hell, not what I was expecting to hear."

"We are already aware of the plot, Brompton."

Ashworth turned to Rathbourne. "We are?"

Derrick nodded at Ashworth, who threw back the rest of the brandy.

"You did well to bring the plot to my attention, Brompton. You must not tell anyone, including Mrs. Brompton, about it. She is too attached to my wife, and if she perceives any threat against the baby, she will not be able to hide it from Henrietta."

"Yes, my lord. I will not inform my wife."

"Escort Lisette and her brother in. And once I've spoken to the siblings, I will summon you to inform you of how our plan will impact the household."

"Sir, you may depend on me to protect the babe with my life."

Rathbourne's face softened, and for possibly the first time, he walked next to the retainer to the door. "Thank you, Brompton. I do not plan for it to come to such a desperate act, but I appreciate your loyalty."

Ashworth strode to Derrick. "Fill me in quickly."

"Edward overheard the plot to kidnap the babe when he was in the woods. Obviously Rathbourne already knew who in his household was part of the plan, since he didn't show any reaction to the French siblings' request. I think he had planned to trap them before they could come forward."

"And here I was being delighted that we found Edward. Can't we have one day without any plots and treachery?"

CHAPTER TWELVE

Amelia's carriage pulled into the elaborate portico of Bonnington estate. She stared at the multiple gleaming windows, sparkling in anticipation of tomorrow's ball. The artist in her appreciated the perfect symmetry of the red brick Georgian estate, with its central entrance and elegant portico.

As a young girl, she always imagined her ancestors' guests arriving for a ball in elaborate panniers, piled hairstyles replete with birds, and secretive masks covered in feathers and jewels. She always felt she should have been born in that era of romantic intrigue and drama, but, after the past few days, she had learned she preferred being part of the current era, part of the fight against the French.

She no longer cared about her ball gown or the flowers. Instead, she wanted to help Cord and Ash prevent baby Charles's kidnapping. How her expectations of a perfect wedding had shriveled and wafted away.

She climbed out of the carriage, steeling herself to greet family and guests who had already arrived for tomorrow's wedding. What she really wanted was to sneak past the drawing room and collapse on her bed. After Hen's labor and the search for Edward, she was exhausted, but also edgy and nervous about the newest threat. She needed a hot bath and a nap before her appearance at tonight's dinner party, hosted by her father in her and Derrick's honor.

She had envisioned this day for months—the overflowing, fragrant flowers, the unique and delicious menu, the guest rooms planned to the last detail for luxury and comfort, playing the role of a sparkling hostess for the arriving guests.

But all that mattered now was keeping Hen's baby safe. And despite the men's reassurance that they would apprehend the wicked monster, she wanted to help in tonight's capture.

She had stayed with Edward for hours, hours when she was supposed to be entertaining the guests. But even then he hadn't wanted her to leave, so she remained with him until he fell asleep.

Her absence from her home was conspicuous. She planned to spend the day enjoying her large family and the many friends who traveled a great distance to attend the wedding.

Derrick had no family, since he was estranged from his brother, and always spoke of Amelia and Aunt Mabel as his only family. He sacrificed his good name in society to spare Lauren, the woman he saved from marriage to his abusive brother, the Marquess of Falconbridge.

Jarvis opened the door. "Miss Amelia, I'm grateful you've arrived. You're needed in the library at once. Master Jack is shouting at one of the guests."

Amelia stared at Jarvis as if he were Medusa holding up a butchered head. Arguments were nothing new in the Bonnington household, as Jarvis was well aware. Growing up with men, Amelia was accustomed to angry bouts of shouting which were usually followed by a round of fisticuffs and ended with broken furniture.

"At a guest?" Amelia shook her head. She didn't have time

for her pig-headed brother's fights. "I'm not going to intervene between Jack and one of his friends, most likely arguing over a horse."

"Miss Amelia, he was shouting at a lady, Lady Mac Allister's sister, Miss Abigail."

For the first time in two days, Amelia burst out in laughter. Jack, the epitome of male confidence and control, was actually shouting at a lady, a guest in their home. This she had to witness. Suddenly not feeling the least bit tired, she followed Jarvis to the library.

Miss Abigail Lyon, upon meeting her ruggedly handsome and rakish brother last year, hadn't been charmed and hadn't swooned over his good looks. Possibly the first woman ever to remain so unaffected by said charm and looks.

Miss Abigail, her wild curls held back with a bright blue bandeau, and dressed in a simple muslin dress, stood near the wall of books, her arms folded across her chest. "My point exactly. And if you read Elizabeth Montague, you would understand, from a woman's point of view, that marriage is an expedient convention with very little advantage."

"Miss Abigail, how lovely to see you've arrived," Amelia greeted her guest. "Jack, I had hoped to find you in the drawing room, entertaining our guests."

Jack, spared Amelia's carrot top hair color, had hair the color of rich mahogany. But he was plagued with fair skin that betrayed his emotions. At this moment, his face was a fiery red.

"Brinsley's Aunt Mabel is in charge. She has taken over the tasks of hostess, and directed me to fetch Miss Lyon for afternoon tea before the ladies retire to prepare for tonight's dinner."

Amelia had been too distracted with the events of the day to consider asking the socially powerful and connected dowager to step into the role of hostess. Of course Aunt Mabel could easily manage Amelia's rambunctious brothers and the society ladies. Aunt Mabel could wage her own war against Napoleon if need be. And, of course, Aunt Mabel was matchmaking when she sent Jack to find Miss Abigail.

"How interesting that you and Jack are discussing the merits of marriage. And how fitting the day before my wedding."

Miss Lyon curtsied. "My deepest apologies, I don't mean that your marriage…"

Jack glowered at Amelia, as if she could be intimidated by a clash between their matching violet eyes. If their positions were reversed, he would not have been able to resist baiting her, either.

"Your brother…" Miss Abigail stopped suddenly. "I shall return to the drawing room."

"Coward," Jack muttered under his breath, but loud enough to be heard.

"Of all the nerve." Miss Abigail's chest puffed out in indignation.

Jack's focus on Miss Abigail's face was diverted to her expanding cleavage. "Don't spare my sister." He stalked Miss Abigail against the wall of books. "She is not missish. Tell her the opinion that you were so willing to share but moments ago."

Miss Lyon looked sheepishly at Amelia. "I have apologized to your brother for my lack of refinement. I'm not sure what came over me."

"Jack came over you. He has that effect on many people."

"You're not helping, Amelia," Jack warned.

Amelia moved closer to Miss Abigail. "What did Jack do this time to vex you so?"

Amelia tried not to sound like she was gloating, but knew she failed from the way Jack's eyes narrowed.

"Your brother's refusal to open his mind to the possibility of women attending university and not marrying is exasperating and illogical."

Miss Abigail shook her blond curls, clearly having no idea what an enticing picture she presented to Jack. Amelia knew by the way Jack watched the fiery woman's every move that he was captivated.

"And you consider yourself an intelligent man..." Miss Abigail shrugged in defeat, turning to Amelia. "Your brother's inability to comprehend that there are women who might not wish to spend their futures with a husband is pitiful."

Amelia really needed to tidy herself and attend to her guests, but the arcing sensual tension between these two kept her too engaged to leave. She had been waiting for the right woman to give Jack his comeuppance.

Miss Abigail stepped around Jack. "I beg your pardon, Miss Amelia. I will return to the guests. I've taken enough of your time. I hope your friend, Lady Rathbourne, is feeling well."

"Lady Henrietta regrets she won't be able to attend the wedding ball. But I believe you would enjoy discussing your views with her. She is an inestimable scholar, who reads and writes many languages, including ancient Greek and Latin. And I believe she would have attended university if she had the opportunity."

"I look forward to meeting Lady Rathbourne when her confinement is finished. I'm here for the season at my father's insistence, but I've been making the acquaintances of like-minded women who are more interested in serious study than the frivolities of society."

"I believe you offended my sister, who is known throughout society as an arbiter of fashion, one of the frivolities you speak of so scornfully," Jack challenged.

Amelia had to suppress the laughter boiling up inside her. Jack, every lady's favorite, was behaving considerably very ill-mannered.

Miss Abigail tilted her head toward Amelia, ignoring Jack. "I beg to differ. You are a talented artist. Your father has taken the time to show me your paintings in the family gallery. But, because you are a woman, you are not able to study with the masters or contemplate expressing your talent in ways considered beyond of a woman's purview. No, I respect women who find ways to express their creative abilities despite society's constraints."

Amelia laced her arm through the young woman's and led her to the doors. "Thank you, Miss Abigail. I appreciate your insight. We must discuss this further."

Amelia looked over her shoulder at Jack's thundering glare. "Jack, will you accompany Miss Abigail back to the drawing room? I must tidy myself before seeing the guests."

Jack offered his arm, and the gleam in his eyes was very familiar to Amelia. Poor Miss Abigail had no clue that she had just thrown down a gauntlet. And none of her brothers ever stepped away from a challenge, especially Jack.

"Thank you, Mr. Bonnington, but I am capable of returning to the drawing room without escort."

Yes, Miss Abigail had no clue what a tempting dare she presented.

"Of all the stubborn women." He bowed as if in the presence

of the king. "Miss Lyon, it would give me pleasure to accompany you to the drawing room."

Miss Abigail rolled her eyes before placing her hand on Jack's arm as if touching a snake. She batted her eyes at Jack and said in a sweet voice, "Thank you, sir. You are too kind."

CHAPTER THIRTEEN

Flanked by his bride and Aunt Mabel, Derrick greeted the wedding guests. Amelia's face was turned toward her father, giving Derrick a perfect view of her slender neck and flame-red hair, which was twisted into complicated braids and curls for tonight's ball. None of the guests would guess from the sweet smile on Amelia's face as she greeted her guests that she was terrified for the safety of Lady Henrietta's baby.

He was used to subterfuge and dissembling, but the challenge for straightforward and honest Amelia was tremendous. He found himself tense and edgy, not because of tonight's mission, but because he was unable to help Amelia, and unable to do anything to protect her from worry.

Amelia had wanted to postpone the ball and assist Rathbourne and Ashworth. He smiled at his brilliant tactics in the face of that challenge. Instead of pointing out that he would never allow her to be involved in a dangerous mission, he tactfully explained that any change in plans would raise suspicion, thus causing the kidnappers to behave rashly.

He had only been married a few hours, and he was already learning how to manage his headstrong wife.

He was normally a man who barely smiled, but he couldn't stop grinning today. Today Amelia, a warm, loving, vivacious woman, bound her life to his, never to be undone. His seemingly endless days of believing he was destined to spend his life alone, afraid that he had inherited the dark, abusive nature of his father and brother, were gone.

Aunt Mabel poked him in the ribs to remind him to attend to the debutante who stood before him stammering and staring. Derrick smiled warmly at the shy young woman, who immediately blushed a deep shade of red that matched the dratted vest Amelia wanted him to wear tonight.

While the girl drifted down the line, Aunt Mabel declared in her loud voice, "You might have damaged the poor gel for life. I thought she was going to have a fainting spell on the spot. Better to save all your charm for your beautiful bride, or we'll have a room filled with women swooning at the sight of Lord Brinsley, amiable and smiling."

"Have you already been in the champagne?" Derrick asked.

"If only. Standing for hours is taking a toll on my feet and back. I remain upright only because I can see we have but a few more guests to greet. Whose idea was it to invite all of London?"

Derrick managed not to remind Aunt Mabel that it was she who expanded the guest list. She wanted all of society to acknowledger her nephew's triumphant return to their midst, and his spectacular match.

"You did very well, marrying Amelia. She's got pluck, and won't let you ride roughshod over her, since she is skillful at managing her father and brothers."

Derrick turned to watch Amelia take an older gentleman's hands in hers, gracing him with her warmth. The gentleman looked besotted by her, as well he should be. She was smiling, and would periodically steal a glance at Derrick. Thanks to her charming smile, he might be the only one in the room to have noticed that her eyes were wide with anxiety. Her distress ratcheted up his uneasiness.

Aunt Mabel dragged his thoughts away from his bride. "Your mother would have loved her. I'm sorry Lucy didn't live to see what a fine match you've made."

Derrick also wished his mother could have met Amelia. How happy she would have been to know one of her sons had found an intelligent, socially adept wife, able to hold her own in a marriage, thus ending the brutal family legacy.

He still didn't trust that he could relax into his present good fortune after the years of isolation and societal rejection. He had believed he was destined to remain alone, and the conviction still haunted him, despite evidence to the contrary.

"I thank my lucky stars that you inherited your mother's gentle nature, and not your father's terrible temperament."

Derrick stared down at the wizened face of his aunt, her dark, beady eyes piercing into his.

"No, don't look at me like I'm batty."

Aunt Mabel was anything but batty. She was sharp and observant. But her description of him as "gentle" was not a word he would have used. Intimidating, dark, menacing were closer to the mark.

"You were always a sweet child, wanting to protect your mother from your father's violent outbursts. You protected Lauren, ruining your rightful place in society. Your wife knows you're a wonderful man. I see it every time she steals a glance at you."

He shook his head.

Aunt Mabel cackled. "Don't worry, my boy, your secret is

safe. I wouldn't want to ruin your reputation as a big, bad, bully boy."

Amelia turned at the sound of Aunt Mabel's laughter. "I believe we are finished with the receiving line. I'm sorry you had to stand for so long, Aunt Mabel."

Derrick looked through the open doors. The line that had snaked down the long, marble hallway for hours had vanished.

"You are not expecting any additional guests? What about Gabby's brother, the dead marquis who was to make his reappearance at your wedding? I was looking forward to the drama."

"Gabby is disappointed that her brother didn't return from France in time to attend," Amelia said.

What Amelia didn't add was that she and Derrick were both grateful for no further intrigue. The kidnapping of an innocent was problematic enough, without a missing spy. But at the moment, there was nothing to be done but enjoy their wedding. And he was going to do everything in his power to ensure Amelia had wonderful memories of the evening she had been planning for months.

"Fiddlesticks, I wanted to see Emily Billingsworth's face when Valmont made his grand entrance." Aunt Mabel lifted her lorgnette to scan the ballroom. "It looks like your ball will still be the talk of the ton. It's a grand squeeze."

"Excuse us, Aunt Mabel. I wish a moment with my wife."

"I'm sure you do." Aunt Mabel winked. "Take your time, and I'll distract the crowd. And why is that annoying French designer still lurking in our vicinity?"

Derrick followed Aunt Mabel's look to where Pisspot stood half-concealed by the red- and purple- and gold-draped column.

Amelia had shared that mixing the bold colors was quite daring, and not normally considered fitting for a wedding. He assumed his wife's talent for bold had been successful, since he heard many compliments from the guests.

"I'm sure he is checking on the ballroom to make sure everything is running smoothly, Aunt Mabel. He's very fastidious about details."

Derrick had the wisdom not to comment on Pisspot or his affectations.

"I don't trust that Frenchie. Something about him ain't right. And I don't mean his manners. Something else."

Derrick agreed, but since Amelia held Pierpont in high esteem, he said nothing. He tucked Amelia's arm into his and led her away from the ballroom into a nook he spotted earlier, planning to steal a kiss from his luscious wife before the next round of socializing and dancing began.

"This is the first chance I've had alone with my wife. And I'm going to take a moment to enjoy my newly wedded bliss." He liked how the sound of "wife" made his possessive male heart beat wildly.

Tucked into the tiny space, he ran his finger along the sensitive spot on the inside of her elbow above her long evening glove, moving closer, wanting to kiss her pale shoulders. "You are the most beautiful bride."

Amelia looked up at him, her face radiant. "You're not upset by my dress?" She lightly ran her hand down the length of the deep purple dress clinging to every curve, so tight that it looked like it might be hard for her to breathe.

Derrick chose not to mention that when she descended the stairwell, his first reaction was the urge to rush up the stairs and drag her to the bedroom, and then his next urge was to shout out that she change into a modest dress that would hide her stunning body to all but his eyes.

What had stopped him was the way Amelia chewed on her lower lip while she carefully descended the stairs, her eyes open and vulnerable, waiting for his approval. She might be the fashion expert in terms of color and design, but as a man, a lusty man who loved her, he understood that her dress was meant as a seduction for him, and only him. What a lucky devil he was. What more could a husband ask?

"You look…" He felt like the big lummox that he was, unable to express what he was feeling. He could only tell her the truth. "I can't think of any pretty words to describe how beautiful you are, and how grateful I am that you belong to me. And only me."

"Lord Derrick Brinsley, I will never forget that you have said such lovely things to me on our wedding night. I'll be old and gray and still telling the grandchildren how dashing and romantic you are."

With the mention of grandchildren, Amelia's smile vanished. "How can I be celebrating when Cord and Ash are searching for someone who is plotting to harm tiny Charles?"

The hell with propriety and the guests in the hallway, Derrick pulled Amelia against him. "Because you are supposed to be thinking of your wedding, not a French threat. It is what Rathbourne and Ashworth want. And you must trust them to do their job. They are well trained and skillful, as are the men accompanying them."

Amelia melted against him and spoke against his chest. "It was hard not to be able to reassure Cord when he came through the receiving line. He looked stressed and alone. It would have broken Hen's heart to see him in that moment."

Rathbourne made an appearance early in the evening to maintain the ruse. After the evening's work, he planned to return to his wife and baby. Ashworth planned to bring the news once the men were captured.

"I saw Aunt Euphemia whispering to you. Did she give you any more information?"

"She told me not to worry. All is under control. I admire her. She is with the men, helping them to stop the villain."

"She certainly is something different." Derrick preferred Amelia to admire Aunt Euphemia from afar. "Cord shared that it was his aunt who was able to convince Lisette to play her part by wrapping the receiving blanket around clothes rolled together to be the same size as the baby."

"The poor girl must be terrified. She is barely sixteen, and has been imprisoned and threatened with her mother's death. I can't imagine what it must be like for her."

"She and her brother did the right thing in coming forward. Rathbourne will make sure her mother is not taken by Fouche, and Adrien will leave with Talley at first light to move his mother beyond Fouche's reach."

A footman approached Derrick. "My Lord, I am sorry to interrupt, but he insisted it was important."

"Who insisted?"

"A French man, Adrien, who said you will know who he is. He says it was vital he speak with you."

Derrick's calm vanished. His muscles clenched and his breath quickened. "Where is he?" Derrick searched the long hallway filled with wandering guests.

Nothing made sense about Adrien's appearance at the ball, nothing except that something had gone wrong, very wrong.

"He is waiting in the garden below the stairs." The footman

nodded toward the open French doors across the ballroom leading to the terrace.

"Derrick, what's happened?" Amelia's voice quavered. "Why does he want to see you? Isn't Ash supposed to arrive soon?"

"I'm sure it's nothing. Ashworth probably sent him ahead, since it will take him longer to return to his estate and change clothes. I'll only be a minute. You return to our guests. Promise me you won't worry."

Amelia searched his face, as if she suspected that he wasn't telling her the whole truth. It made no sense for Adrien, a stable hand, to search for him amongst the wedding guests. He hoped Amelia wouldn't catch on.

"Something is wrong. Adrien wouldn't summon you at your ball."

This was the problem with having an intelligent wife. "We can't both leave the ball. Remember, we're not to draw attention. You must take up your role as the new bride." Derrick couldn't stop the sense of dread raising the little hairs on the back of his neck. "I saw your brother Jack talking with Miss Lyon. Will you go be with your brother until I return?"

"You believe something is wrong, too. Otherwise you wouldn't want me to be with Jack." Amelia tightened the hold on his arm.

"I'm a spy. I always believe something is wrong. It's my nature. Most likely it is exactly as I said, Ashworth will arrive later, and wants to notify us of their success."

Amelia dropped his arm and pulled her shoulders back. "I'll return to the ball, but I choose to worry until I hear that nothing has gone awry and the villains have been apprehended."

He pressed a kiss to her warm lips in quick reassurance for both of them. "I won't be long. And I can't wait for tonight, when I get to unwrap the perfect purple present you created for your husband."

Amelia flushed while she bit her lower lip. At least he had succeeded in distracting her, but he didn't like the way his gut was twitching. He'd learned from years of experience to trust his instincts. Something was wrong, brutally wrong, by the way his body and heartbeat ratcheted into battle mode.

CHAPTER FOURTEEN

Derrick hurried along the side of the crowded ballroom, trying to avoid conversations with his guests. No one approached him. Most likely his explosive scowl warned them off.

He rushed down the steps into the formal garden lit with lanterns for the balmy fall night, and next turned off the pathway to the right, as the footman instructed.

Adrien stepped immediately out of the shadows. "Lord Brinsley, I'm sorry to interrupt you tonight. But it is most important."

"What has happened?" Tension shot through Derrick's body at the jumpy way the young man moved toward him.

"Lord Ashworth sent a note to inform you that the mission has been accomplished. He wants you and Lady Brinsley not to worry. We've succeeded in capturing Chasen and his accomplice."

A wave of relief washed through him at the news for the sake of both Rathbourne and Amelia. He wanted nothing to upset her on this night. He curbed his need to ask if Rathbourne had beaten Chasen to a bloody mess. He would wait for the details from Ashworth.

"Then why all this subterfuge?" At his severe tone, Adrien took a step back.

"Lord Ashworth was very clear that I was to give the note only to Mr. Jarvis, Bonnington's butler. When I arrived at the servants' quarters, a footman led me upstairs to the dining room, where Mr. Jarvis was directing the servants for the late-night supper.

Derrick tried to curb his impatience with the young man who was barely eighteen years old. Tonight must not have been easy for him. Adrien had shown courage to sacrifice himself to protect his mother and sister. It wasn't lost on Derrick that Adrien followed the same path as Derrick had to protect the innocent.

"There was a very stylish Frenchman in the dining room speaking with Mr. Jarvis. At first I thought he was a guest, since he was wearing a fine coat and jewels. But there was something familiar about him, the way he gestured with his hands. Then I realized he was on the same boat as Lisette and me. I came up on the deck late at night, and saw him in conversation with the man who called himself Chasen, the man who brought us from France. Chasen works for Fouche. They were hiding behind the fishing nets, looking around to make sure they were not noticed."

"That bastard. I'm going to kill him." A familiar rage coursed through Derrick's body, the same sensation as when he was subjected to his father's outbursts—a need to retaliate and destroy. As a young man, this killing fury had convinced him that he was a savage monster like his father. Over time, he learned to control his response to his father's cruelty, and then how to temper his reactions in the world at large.

He wanted to swear, and rage, and punch his fist into Pisspot's soft gut. Instead, he reminded himself that he had sworn to only use his power to defend the weak and the unprotected. And by God, Amelia was the unprotected, and it was totally his fault.

Derrick swallowed the ferocity bubbling up. "He calls himself Pierpont. Did you hear anything they were saying?"

Adrien shook his head. "No. I couldn't risk having Chasen notice me on the deck."

"Did you ever see the men together again?"

"Only when we were leaving the boat. The man nodded to Chasen before he got into a fancy carriage and drove off."

Derrick had to get to Amelia, and then he was going to take Pierpont apart. Or whatever the hell the weasel's name was.

"Get this information to Lord Rathbourne immediately. Tell him I have enough men to assist me. I will send Pierpont to London once I'm finished with him."

Before beating Pierpont to a bloody pulp, he needed to extract the Frenchman's real purpose in entangling himself in Amelia's life.

"Yes, my lord. I'll deliver the message immediately." Adrien bowed.

Derrick turned and stopped mid-step. "Thank you, Adrien for informing me of the traitor. And you've done a fine job protecting your sister and your mother."

Derrick hurried to the stairs while sifting through various dangerous scenarios. Incomprehensible—Pierpont, a French agent sent by Fouche, spending endless hours with Amelia. His entire being was stretched tight and taut, ready for action.

Why hadn't he trusted his suspicions? Because Amelia wanted to work with the creative genius who was rumored to have been one of Josephine Bonaparte's favorites. And he wanted Amelia happy. Pierpont's story had checked out. And, distracted with the Irish threat, Derrick had not delved deep enough. Guilt for allowing Pierpont into Amelia's life would hound him forever.

But now the challenge—how to extract the bastard from the ballroom without Amelia's notice. The pisspot was probably going to start screaming or crying when he realized Derrick had found him out.

Derrick thundered up the stairs and into the ballroom. Standing at the door, he scanned the crowded ballroom for Amelia. Grateful for his height, he was able to see over the heads of all the guests. There was no sign of his bride or the Frenchman in the sea of people. Derrick wished to hell the betrayal was not going to devastate her, but first he must make certain that Pierpont didn't harm her. How could Amelia's perfect night be shattered? And where was she?

He refused to give in to the desperate fear skirting on the edges of his mind, making his hands shake and his body tremble.

Pierpont had no clue that his cover was blown. Amelia was safe.

Realizing that many in the crowded room had turned at his entrance and were staring at him, Derrick took a deep breath and nodded formally. He needed to pull himself together, and not draw attention and alert Pierpont to his danger.

He pasted a smile of sorts on his face and pushed his way through the guests. "Excuse me, needed by my wife."

He heard a few men chuckle and offer their sympathy. "Poor dog."

It took all his discipline to not shove harder. If he wanted to, he could clear the room in seconds. He lost his smile and polite manner halfway across the enormous room. He caught the comments that were intentionally loud enough for him to hear. "Already marital problems…" "Told you the happiness was all an act… Miss Bonnington was always in love with Lord Kendal."

Derrick gritted his teeth and dodged two gossiping matrons before finally making it to the other side of the ballroom. Amelia was not in the entranceway with her brother and Miss Lyon. She had promised she would join them.

Derrick barked at the two footmen who stood at the doors. "Where is my wife?"

The footman stiffened. "My lord, Mr. Pierpont informed her ladyship that Cook had fallen and broken her leg. Lady Brinsley was very upset and went to the kitchen."

The bastard had Amelia. How had Pierpont discovered the threat? Derrick ran toward the servants' quarters. He shouted back to the footmen. "Was anyone else with her?"

"No, my lord. Only Mr. Pierpont."

Derrick didn't take the time to gather his men, who were scattered throughout the estate. He wasn't going to waste a second. He would take care of Pierpont himself with his bare hands.

Derrick barreled around the corner of the long hallway. Amelia and the snake were walking together. "Amelia." Derrick didn't want to give any indication to Pierpont, but he heard the desperation in his voice.

Amelia turned. "Darling, what has happened?" She began to rush to Derrick when Pierpont grabbed her arm. The usually languid bastard was certainly fast and efficient when he grabbed Amelia.

Stunned, Amelia tripped and turned toward the Frenchman. "Pierpont, what are you doing? You're hurting my arm."

Pierpont pulled out a sharp stiletto from his boot. "He knows."

Derrick considered rushing Pierpont, but the cornered man might stab Amelia.

"Have you gone mad? Release me now." Amelia twisted, trying to break his grip on her arm.

Derrick clenched his fists at his side. "Let her go, and I'll go easy on you. If you harm her, I will slowly tear you apart."

Pierpont yanked Amelia's back against his chest and pressed the glimmering knife against her pale throat.

Pierpont was going to suffer and wish he had never touched Amelia with violent intent.

"She'll be dead before you can reach her."

Pierpont's maniacal laugh froze Derrick and forced him to stillness. Derrick prayed no one came out of the servants' quarters and forced Pierpont to react.

"Derrick, will you please explain why Pierpont is holding a knife to my throat?" Amelia, trying hard to be brave, heightened Derrick's frantic urgency to free her and abolish Pierpont.

"Release her, and you can go."

Pierpont laughed again in a high-pitched cackle. "As if you don't intend to hunt me down."

"On my gentleman's honor, I will not hunt you. But only if you let her go unharmed." Derrick didn't mention that he wouldn't prevent Rathbourne and Ashworth from pursuing the traitor.

"Miss Amelia, I'm sorry. It wasn't supposed to happen this way." He sneered at Derrick. "I will kill her if you don't allow me to leave. I've killed many, and it is of no consequence."

Amelia was staring at Derrick as if she were hatching an idea to break away. Derrick glared at Amelia, trying to convey "Don't you dare" with his steely glower.

"I have a horse waiting at the servants' quarters. And once I've left the estate, I will deposit Miss Amelia on the road. If your men follow me or shoot at me, she is a dead woman. Do I make myself clear?"

"Yes. I'll adhere to your plan." Derrick put his arms in the air as an act of surrender. "Do not harm her. She has done nothing."

Knowing that Pierpont was desperate, Derrick forced his voice to a quiet calm. "Amelia, do exactly as he asks."

He hoped she would not try anything. Knowing Amelia, she was already considering ways to disarm him.

"You go ahead. I don't want you behind me." Pierpont pointed to the door.

Derrick opened the delivery door to the outside. A horse was tethered to a post.

"Walk outside slowly. And don't consider shouting for help."

Amelia gasped when Pierpont pressed the blade harder against her throat. "One little slice, right here at the artery, and your wife will bleed to death."

Derrick kept his hands at his side, not wanting to incite the lunatic into a rash act.

"Amelia, I will collect you on the road after Pierpont makes his escape. There is nothing to be worried about."

How Pierpont planned to mount the horse with Amelia in an evening gown, he didn't know, but it opportunity Derrick was waiting for. If Pierpont lifted her onto the horse, he would have to turn his back to Derrick.

But the gleam in Pierpont's eyes conveyed that he had deduced Derrick's plan.

Pierpont turned Amelia with her back to Derrick. "If you make a move, I'll still have time to gut her."

Amelia flinched. Derrick stood perfectly still, painfully aware of how dangerous Pierpont had become.

"What a shame, Miss Amelia, that you've become my means of escape. I've enjoyed our time together." He slashed Amelia's dress at her knee with the sharp blade, tugging at the material until Amelia's legs were now exposed to her silk drawers. The bastard was going to suffer for the indignities inflicted on Derrick's precious bride.

Amelia snorted. "I should have suspected when I realized you have no sense of color or design."

Pierpont grabbed Amelia's arm. "Mount the horse, and no tricks. I know you to be a skilled rider."

Amelia gave Derrick the innocent, wide-eyed look he recognized from cricket matches. She was going to do something very risky and very stupid.

"Amelia, do you trust me to protect you?"

"Of course, darling." Why didn't Derrick feel reassured by her response? He leaned forward, ready to dive between Amelia and the knife.

"Shut up and get on the horse."

Derrick would have a small window, an instant of time, to jump on Pierpont when Amelia was out of the direct path of the blade while Pierpont mounted the horse. Derrick readied himself mentally to grab the slimy bastard, then held his breath and waited.

Amelia placed her foot into the stirrup and then threw herself up into the saddle with a great leap, then sliding over the top of the horse and landing on the gravel.

Before Pierpont could react, Derrick leapt forward and threw a solid punch to the villain's face, holding nothing back. Pierpont folded like a deflated balloon and crumpled to the ground. Derrick bent over the unconscious man. It had been too easy, and not very satisfying to knock him out, stone cold, with one punch. Derrick retrieved the knife from the ground.

Amelia tethered the horse's reins back to the post.

"Amelia, are you hurt?" Derrick rushed to her and pulled her into his arms.

"I'm fine." She trembled against him with tiny shivers. He could feel her galloping heart against his chest.

Derrick released her, only to remove his coat and wrap it around her, before tugging her back into his arms.

"I am never going to forget…" Derrick couldn't finish. The words were wedged in his throat, strangling him with fear. He couldn't consider the possibility of losing her. "And what were you thinking, taking such a risk? Of all the insane ideas."

Amelia snuggled closer and hugged him around the waist. "I knew you'd make toast of Pierpont if you had a chance."

Derrick laughed loud in relief that his beloved Amelia was safe.

"And I was right." Amelia looked back at the unconscious man. "But what was Pierpont's purpose in ingratiating himself as a design protégé? And is Lady Wadsworth a French spy, too? I am at sixes and sevens."

Derrick recognized Amelia's chatter as a release of nerves like a greenhorn after his first battle. "Let's get you inside and away from this scum."

Amelia pulled out of his arms and stepped around Pierpont, who lay motionless on the ground, and picked up the fabric from her gown. "I don't want anyone to find the silk and speculate about how my dress was slashed to shreds. There is going to be enough gossip when I return to the ball in a different gown."

"You are not going to return to the ball. You need to rest. A French assassin just held you at knifepoint."

"There is no need for concern. I knew you'd save me."

Derrick was grateful for her faith in his ability, but he knew how quickly Pierpont could have delivered a deathblow. He didn't want to think about how close he came to losing her. It would be a long time before he forgot this night. If ever.

Amelia rose on her toes and kissed his cheek. "Returning to the ball will help us both forget this unfortunate episode. And I refuse to have bad memories of my wedding ball. I want to dance."

"Fuck the ball. We are leaving for my estate. Go change your clothes."

"Derrick Brinsley, did you just use that word in my presence?" And she giggled. She wasn't as collected as she was trying to pretend.

"I'm going upstairs to change into another gown, while you do whatever you do to get rid of this…this traitor." She shook her head. "And to think I trusted him."

"I apologize, Amelia, for my language, but I'm not interested in anything but keeping you safe and away from harm."

"Darling, please, I want to dance with you at our ball. You promised me."

"How can you care about a damn dance? We'll go to plenty of balls."

"We'll never have our wedding ball again, and I refuse to allow French spies to ruin my night."

Derrick realized he should be grateful that Amelia wasn't falling apart. She had worked hard to create the perfect wedding ball for them both, for months. He resigned himself to dancing and socializing. "Aunt Mabel was right about you. You have pluck. I'll give you that, but from now on, no more damn French anything. Do I make myself clear?"

"Yes, dear." Amelia, wrapped in his coat, rushed through the door. "I'll meet you in the ballroom in less than twenty minutes. What thrilling stories we'll be able to tell our children and grandchildren about our wedding ball."

EPILOGUE

Amelia locked fingers with her husband's. She tested the word silently—*husband*. Yes. Derrick truly belonged to her. In the black night, she looked up at the large figure towering over her. Derrick was as solid, straight, and true as the giant oaks looming above them.

Light from the lantern swinging in Derrick's hand accentuated the hard angles of his broad face.

In the silent woods, she could feel the quiet tension radiating from him. After the ball, he had been brusque, directing her to dress warmly, since they would be walking to a surprise rendezvous for their wedding night. Since it was the wee hours of the night, she had assumed that they would spend their wedding night at her father's estate.

Derrick wasn't a man of surprises. He was a quiet, serious man like her father.

Her world had been tilted on its axis many times in the past few days.

Nothing about the wedding had turned out as planned, including the revelation that her assistant wasn't a friend or a design expert, but a French assassin sent to kill Gabby's brother for revenge.

Amelia felt the burn of embarrassment, almost shame, like a

sunburn on her sensitive skin. She had always believed herself to be a good judge of character, observant, possessing spy skills like her husband, since she had helped to expose a French smuggling ring the previous year.

She felt ignorant and ashamed by how naïve she had been. She knew nothing of the lengths men might be willing to go to seek revenge.

The only thing she did know was that she would never again be concerned when everything wasn't perfect. Life wasn't perfect. And it was messier when you cared.

"Derrick, where are you taking me?"

"If I tell you, it won't be a surprise." Derrick kept a tight grip on her hand.

"But why all the secrecy? You're not expecting another French assassin, are you?" Her attempt to lighten her husband's somber mood fell as flat as a ball hit off the side of the bat for a cheap base hit.

Since the encounter with Pierpont, Derrick exuded a level of tension she had never witnessed in him. He'd returned to the ball after dealing with the French worm, and performed the roles of host and newlywed husband admirably. Only someone who knew him very well could know he was simmering with suppressed emotion.

"I wouldn't put it past your brothers to plan hijinks for our wedding night. In fact, because of the grins I saw on those scoundrels' faces at the end of the ball, I have a feeling it is exactly what they planned. I wish I could see their shock when they discover your empty bedchamber."

Amelia had a pretty good idea where this trail was taking them—they were on their way to the dower house. Her grandmother had lived there after her husband's death, but since her death no one had inhabited the two-story Georgian home.

"My brothers know nothing of your plan?"

"No, only your father and Jarvis, who were both sworn to secrecy. With family and friends always underfoot, we never have any time to ourselves. I want this night to be special, a way for the two of us to begin our marriage.

Amelia's heart beat fast with the ardent promise she heard in Derrick's impassioned voice. She pulled on Derrick's hand, stopping his forward motion. "I'm so glad you had the foresight to plot an escape from my family."

"Speaking of escaping your family…"

Amelia resisted the feeling of guilt that inevitably followed thoughts of leaving her family.

"I have a wedding present for you."

"But you gave me the modiste's as a wedding present."

"But that was months ago, before you were my wife." He pressed an open-mouthed kiss to her palm.

Heated awareness blasted along her spine to the backs of her knees. She went on tiptoe and pressed herself flush against his hard body. "I don't need any gifts—only you."

Derrick wrapped his strong arms around her, holding her close. He whispered into her ear, sending shivers dancing along her skin. "Don't you want to hear what your wedding present is?"

Amelia rubbed against the hard length of him, pressing against her abdomen. "I don't need you to tell me. I can feel it." She giggled.

Derrick's abrupt laugh wafted his warm, lime-scented breath across her face. "What am I going to do with you?"

"I have no idea, but I'm excited to find out. You've been

making promises for weeks now. Let's hurry. I don't want to wait any longer."

Derrick swept her into his arms and proceeded down the trail. "I guess you don't want to hear about your present."

Amelia draped her arms around his neck. "Something to do with my family, who I don't want to think about tonight. I don't want to think about anyone but us." Because of the late night, Derrick had foregone his cravat and his shirt was open. She snuggled closer to him to savor the smell of lime, sage, and the clean, masculine scent of Derrick.

"I purchased the Livingston estate."

Amelia pulled back to get a better look at his face. "You did? But how? Lord Livingston's nephew inherited the estate."

"The nephew isn't interested in rusticating in the country and has gambling debts. And since it wasn't entailed, I purchased it."

"But it means we'll be living close to my family." Tears gathered behind her eyes. She had longed to be close to her father and brothers, hadn't been able to imagine going for months without seeing Drew and Colin, who were more like her children than her siblings.

"You'll be forced to see my father and brothers all the time," she added.

"Well, when you make it sound like that, I might have to change my mind." He shuddered dramatically, getting her to smile. "I know how important you are to your family, and I couldn't bear being the cause of the separation. If I must leave England, I want you to be near to your family and friends."

Amelia's joy deflated in an instant. Derrick might be leaving her. She took a slow breath and tried to recover the elation of the past moment, when the future was bright and hopeful.

"You already have an assignment?" Amelia hated the quiver in her voice. She was proud that her husband was part of his majesty's secret underground, but she certainly didn't want Derrick to leave England and put himself in danger again.

"No, but France has plans to invade Ireland, and I might have to travel north."

"Ireland?"

"It is a possibility. We have to find the ways to protect the entire kingdom from a French invasion."

"Of course you do." She respected Derrick's bravery and loyalty. She understood the need for all English men and women to join in protecting their country. She must not think only of her feelings when so much was at stake. "For tonight, let's not speak of the war."

Derrick swooped her up and spun in a big circle. "I agree wholeheartedly. Tonight we take time for ourselves."

"I like the idea of time simply for us." She nuzzled the tender skin of his throat. "Thank you for planning tonight, and being so thoughtful of my feelings for my family. I'm the luckiest of women."

Derrick tightened his hold on her when Amelia planted soft wet kisses from his neck to his ear. She tugged on his earlobe with her teeth before exploring with her tongue.

Derrick's strong chest heaved like a bellows against her body. Amelia's heart fluttered at the tightening of his muscled arms and the excited sounds of his breathlessness.

She tried to unbutton his shirt one-handed. "You have too many clothes on." She skimmed her hand down the front of his shirt. "I can't wait much longer to be alone with you without your clothes."

"You're incorrigible." He laughed. The deep sound reverberated against her skin.

"I would hope so." Amelia giggled, feeling light with relief to finally be alone with her husband. They had saved themselves from a trained killer, and she would not spend her wedding night worrying about what might threaten them in the future. She was a married woman, and she was happy. She refused to let a little war with France stop her from celebrating tonight.

Derrick quickened his pace. "If it weren't so blasted dark, I'd run, oh impatient wife of mine." She liked hearing the lilt of happiness in his voice.

They came around the curve in the trail to the driveway leading to the dower house. Candles were lit throughout the house, shining into the darkness, lighting their way.

"Are the servants here?" Amelia didn't want to think about having tomorrow's breakfast served by Jarvis, who had been with the Bonningtons since she was a little girl.

"No, they've all gone back to the mansion."

Amelia stretched up to kiss Derrick. He lifted her higher while his head descended. Their lips met and clung.

Derrick pulled away. "We need to get to the bedroom."

She was breathless, tingling with anticipation.

With Amelia in his arms, Derrick opened the front door and ascended the stairs to the bedroom chamber. Candles illuminated the length of the winding hallway.

"I love your primitive approach, but I could walk to let you save your strength for more important matters," she whispered over the sound of her heart thumping loudly in her ears.

Derrick reached around to open the door to the bedroom. A fire blazed in the hearth, the heavy damask covers were pulled down on the bed, and a table was set near the window. The silver cloth-covered table held an open bottle of champagne, sparkling glasses, an assortment of cheeses, meats, and bread, and a bouquet of the same red roses which graced their wedding and ball.

"This is perfect. When did you have time to plan all of this?"

Keeping her pressed against him, Derrick slowly lowered her, rubbing her against his hard, aroused body.

"Jarvis did all the work. All I told him was to have champagne and roses, since I know how much you love them both. But he must have realized that we would be hungry after the long ball."

Amelia wrapped her arms around Derrick's middle, holding onto the brave man who had become her husband. "I'm hungry only for you."

Amelia had anticipated this moment—when Derrick told her at the ball that he couldn't wait to unwrap her as his gift of a lifetime.

She had changed out of her walking dress after her maid left her, and into a French concoction she had designed especially for tonight. A nightgown of white silk with tiny satin ribbons that held the plunging neckline together, and a silk dressing gown that wasn't for warmth, but simply for its sheer, sumptuous fabric. Her heart thrashed as heat crept up her skin.

He bent to untie her cloak. "Let's get rid of this…"

With his closeness, Amelia could see his face flush with color and hear the quick catch in his breath.

"My God, Amelia." His voice was raw, almost strangled.

His passionate desire fed hers, setting her heart into a whizzing rhythm.

He clutched her upper arms, moving her closer to the fire and into the light. Feeling self-conscious under Derrick's slow and careful perusal, she didn't know where to look. "My own design. What do you think?"

"I would have sprinted in the dark if I had known what was waiting for me." Derrick's attention focused on her breasts caused her nipples to tighten as if he were touching her.

Derrick lifted her into his arms again. This was becoming a habit with her husband—carrying her in a prehistoric, possessive way. He set her next to the bed, pulled her hard against him, and took her mouth with a desperate hunger.

She answered the demand in his rising need. Suddenly she was in the arms of a primitive being who wanted her with a passion she had never imagined, much less experienced. But she wasn't frightened by his vehement demands. She was enthralled. Alive, liberated in her feminine power.

She kissed him back, surrendering to his hunger. His desperate kiss found a desperate response in her.

"Amelia, I could have lost you tonight. I can't stop replaying that moment when Pisspot held the knife next to your throat. I'll never forgive myself for placing you in danger."

He was kneading her bottom, pulling her against his manly parts grinding himself against her. "My God, what if I had lost you?"

He always appeared so sure of himself, a man who would never admit to fear or fright, in command of every situation. His love and need moved her as never before. She stopped thinking of herself and thought only of him.

"I'm sorry," she panted, barely able to speak. "I was afraid, too. If anything happened to you, I wouldn't want to go on living."

She felt the strong shudder of his body against hers as she fastened her lips desperately to his and clung to him. If he was upset, so was she. He was only a man, a man who couldn't stop a knife or bullet.

"We need to get out of these clothes. Too many damn clothes, and I need you so badly." Derrick tore off his waistcoat, pulled his shirt over his head and threw it aside.

Amelia followed, discarding her dressing gown.

Derrick knelt and kissed along the border of her neckline. His tongue traced the lace while he undid the ribbons. The backs of his knuckles brushed against her hot skin, eliciting cascades of goose bumps.

Amelia ran her hands over the dark hair covering the muscled wall of his chest.

He trembled with her touch. "I need you."

He spread the nightgown apart and took her breasts into his hands, squeezing the sensitive mounds. Amelia gasped before leaning into his touch.

He circled her nipple with his fingertip before taking it into his mouth. The heat and arousal overwhelmed her, making her weak, as if she might faint.

Derrick moved to her other nipple and sucked hard. She threw back her head in abandonment, spreading her feet apart, since she felt her legs buckling. "I need to lie down.

His eyes were dark, his breathing shallow and quick.

He lifted her nightgown over her head. She gasped with the cool air and his ravenous stares. "Don't be shy with me, Amelia. I'm your husband."

She dug her fingers into his hard shoulders, wanting to be close to the fire radiating off his strong chest while he lifted her onto the bed.

Derrick kicked off his boots, flinging them against the wall, and yanked down his breeches and smalls in one quick motion, his eyes full of sensual promises.

Where she was pale and soft, he was dark and hard and powerful. His broad shoulders tapered to solid, muscular thighs. His sex was long, thick, and jutted from a dark nest of coarse hair. She swallowed hard. She had never seen him unclothed in the bright light. She shook with rising excitement and trepidation.

"Look at me, Amelia. I'm only a man, a man who wants and loves you."

How could she resist him? She opened her arms. "Oh, Derrick. Love me."

He lay next to her and began to caress her again with his lips and tongue, but with less restraint. His arms clamped around her, dragging her as close as they could get. She was carried away by the sheer magnitude of his desire, the wild and wanton demands of his hands and mouth. Primitive needs were becoming unbearable. She arched into him, heedless in her desire.

"Amelia, I can't wait." He spread her legs and entered her, thrusting into her heavily, lunging, filling her completely, and scorching her with waves of pleasure. Her skin was hot, and an ache deep within intensified with his every thrust.

He kissed her fiercely, hotly, then, cupping his hands around her bottom, he lifted her to him and drove into her over and over again, taking them both over into a tumult of light and heat. She trembled in ecstasy, feeling him empty himself into her with deep, hard, convulsive thrusts.

He collapsed onto her, his body enveloping her in heat and sweat. She was light-headed and filled with love. She didn't want anything more than to feel his body pressing her into the softness of the bed.

She ran her hands along his strong back. The smells of Derrick and their lovemaking were new to her, but enveloped her with contentment and a deep sense of safety.

He ran his whiskered chin along her neck, his sex soft and still inside her. She didn't want to move. "Amelia, I promise it will be better next time. I…needed you too damn much after tonight's threat."

Amelia wrapped her arms around his back, melting into him. "If it gets any better, I'll not survive."

His deep-throated chuckle got the response she hoped. She didn't want to relive the betrayal by someone she considered a friend. She wanted to savor the love and passion of her husband.

Derrick rolled off her, but took her with him so she wasn't deprived of his body's warmth. He gently pushed back the hair falling across her face and kissed her lightly. "My fiery redhead. How did I get so lucky? You aren't in the least intimidated by my ardor, are you, my love?"

"Lucky for you, I grew up surrounded by men." Amelia laughed "Well, not that way. You know what I mean."

"I haven't forgotten that you had men around you throughout your childhood. What was Kendal whispering to you at the ball?"

Amelia sat up abruptly. "Really, after this moment?" She didn't have words for what they experienced together tonight, but she recognized love. She threw up her hands in frustration. "How can you possibly still be jealous of Michael?"

He pulled her down next to him, his fingers skimming her arms with tender touches. He wouldn't look her in the eye. "Amelia, you might not be intimidated by men, but you don't understand how men's brains work. We are very simple and possessive. I will never stop being jealous of other men being near to you."

She opened her mouth to protest. But he pressed his finger over her lips. She was tempted to bite it.

"I know you think of Kendal as a friend. And I will tolerate his closeness, but I won't like it…ever. I want to hoard every one of your smiles and touches for me alone."

Amelia stretched half across him, her breasts rubbing against his coarse chest hair. "Michael is a dear childhood friend. And he was teasing me about a secret code."

"Secret code?"

"At first I thought he was serious about a code he had deciphered, but he asked me whether I knew the Wedding Code."

"There is a Wedding Code? This is news to me. What is it?"

"To always hold your love's heart tenderly in your hands."

THE END

THE
CODE BREAKERS
SERIES

"Spies, Intrigue, and a Super Smart heroine. Exactly my type of Regency."
—Rosemary Jones,
Author of *Cold Steel & Spies*

A
Cantata
of Love

JACKI
DELECKI

BESTSELLING AUTHOR

Michael Harcourt, the Earl of Kendal, woke to the soft voice and the delectable smell of a woman. She smelled like wildflowers. And her voice was soothing and sweet. Last night must have been one hell of a night of dissipation since he remembered nothing. He dreamt about his French mother crooning to him.

What was wrong with him? He had been in bed with a French woman and he thought of his mother. His head ached as if horses had trampled over him. He tried to remember her name—Yvette? Or was it Mimi? He cracked open one eye. Big blue eyes the color of cornflowers stared down at him, and a pink lush lower lip was pouting. How could he have forgotten this angel's name? Yvette. Definitely Yvette. "Yvette?" Or maybe Mimi? "Mimi?"

He needed her again to refresh his memory. He raised his arms to pull her against him. He grabbed for her, but his arms felt weak. Thank God the rest of his body wasn't that tired. She yelped when he wrapped his arms around her and pulled her on top of him. "Yvette, darling. Don't fight me. I need you."

Yvette gasped and tightened against him. He rubbed himself against her slender body. Not his usual type he noted. Clearly not an opera dancer by the slender frame. What had he drunk last night that he couldn't remember this delicious handful?

"Let go of me." She hissed.

He whispered against her soft, tender neck, kissing her ear. "Were you this feisty last night?"

"Let me go, you brute." She shouted next in his ear, causing his head to feel as if it were cracking wide open. She jumped back, tripping on the bedclothes and knocking the water canister from the side table. The loud crash reverberated in his head.

Women didn't fight him. He was a generous lover. Obviously he had overlooked something about last night.

Michael looked at the disheveled, beautiful woman glaring at him. Her blond hair sparkled in the morning sunlight, but her bright eyes were now dark and stormy.

Damn, damn. She looked way too innocent and way too marriageable. What had he gotten himself into?

He rearranged the bedding to hide the obvious, then lifted himself to the head of the bed.

The mademoiselle didn't look so much offended as just plain pissing mad. Her eyes had narrowed and her face glowed a deep red. She had the look of a woman who might impale him with the fireplace poker.

The door to his bedroom swung open, knocking against the wall. The pain behind his eyes pounding like a son of a…

Denby, his valet, stormed into the room, swearing under his breath. "What the hell? Are you okay, Mademoiselle Gabrielle?"

She gestured with her hands and spoke in rapid French to Denby. Had she just called the Earl of Kendal a "stupid, horse's ass?"

Denby took the irate woman's arm. "I'll clean up the mess. Now that he's awake, you should prepare yourself to leave. We've a long journey ahead of us."

With no word of farewell, the Mademoiselle Gabrielle huffed and left the room.

Denby chuckled "Barely awake and already causing problems." He bent to pick up the water container. "It is good to see you back, my lord. You scared the hell out of me. If it weren't for Mademesoille Gabby's nursing, I'm not sure…"

"I've been sick?" He did feel a bit weak after his rustle with the young woman.

"You developed a fever right after we escaped from Paris."

The memory of fleeing Paris and Fouche's men brought him totally awake. "All I remember is leaving Paris dressed as a nun."

ABOUT THE AUTHOR

About the Author: Jacki Delecki is a Best-Selling, Romantic Suspense writer. Delecki's **Grayce Walters Series,** which chronicles the adventures of a Seattle animal acupuncturist, was an editor's selection by USA Today. Delecki's Romantic Regency **The Code Breaker Series** hit number one on Amazon. Both acclaimed series are available for purchase at http://www.JackiDelecki.com.

To learn more about Jacki and her books and to be the first to hear about contests and giveaways join her newsletter found on her website: www.JackiDelecki.com. Follow her on FB—Jacki Delecki; Twitter @jackidelecki.